Lock Down Publications and Ca$h
Presents

A

Thuggish Passion

Nothing Like Hood Love

Written By

Ira B

First Edition 2025

Printed in the United States of America

This is a work of fiction. Names, characters, places, and incidents either are products of the author's imagination or are used fictitiously. Any similarity to actual events or locales or persons, living or dead, is entirely coincidental.

Lock Down Publications
P.O. Box 944
Stockbridge, GA 30281
www.lockdownpublications.com

Like our page on Facebook: Lock Down Publications
www.facebook.com/lockdownpublications.ldp

Stay Connected with Us!

Text **LOCKDOWN** to 22828 to stay up-to-date with new releases, sneak peaks, contests and more…

Like our page on Facebook:
Lock Down Publications

Join Lock Down Publications/The New Era Reading Group

Visit our website:
www.lockdownpublications.com

Follow us on Instagram:
Lock Down Publications

Email Us: We want to hear from you!

PROLOGUE

As he looked out from beyond the safety shelter of a local church veranda, all Kaedon could do was shake his head in weary. Of all the things that he could be doing, here he was outside stuck in the middle of a rainstorm. Otherwise, he wouldn't be able to reach the goal he intends to reach if he wasn't.

But with one destination in mind, Kaedon knew there was no other choice but to continue his journey. He'd come thus far in the storm, another mile or two shouldn't be that much of a difficult task.

Given where he came from, Kaedon welcomed the trials ahead of him to reach his destination.

Without further ado, Kaedon braced himself against the driving rain and darted across the back entrance of the big church onto the sidewalk. From there, he allowed the heavy drops of rain to assault his body as he ran up the slick sidewalk.

Overhead, the sky was of a dark gray hue as rain the size of marbles plummeted the earth around Kaedon in a riotous percussion. The downpour was so vicious that in certain areas people's homes were flooding.

Kaedon was running as hard as he could to put distance in between his former location. He would have challenged worse conditions than the rainstorm to escape the living hell had left behind across town.

As he ran as hard as he could run, Kaedon had no clue what was about to transpire next. All he knew was to run and not look back.

But all that changed when suddenly a wrong step on the slick sidewalk twisted his ankle and sent him airborne for a moment before slamming backwards against the wet concrete surface.

"Fuck!" Kaedon bellowed, wincing from pain spurting from his wounded ankle. "Shit, man!" He replied. Kaedon tried to ignore the pain and made an attempt to climb back up to his feet. Once he made it back up to his feet, Kaedon made a move to continue his journey and fell on his ass again.

"This shit can't be happening," Keadon said to himself as he lay flat back against the concrete sidewalk.

In the distance, you could hear police sirens blaring. The driving rain seemed to have picked up a little. To keep the heavy raindrops from continually punching him in the face, Kaedon forced himself to turn sideways.

And that's when he saw her. She was hurrying towards him from the safety of her home. Kaedon closed his eyes for a moment, then he reopened them, and there she was reaching down towards him.

"Are you hurt?" Said the woman.

"My ankle," he said. "I think I twisted it."

"Which one?" She asked.

He pointed down at his left leg.

"Okay. Let's get you up and out of this storm," she replied, taking it upon herself to lift him up to his feet. "You have to help me carry you too, you know?" She added with just a little bit of sass.

"Thank you," Kaedon replied.

And together, with the help of one another, Kaedon was carried off to shelter. But little did he know that this one simple act of kindness would change his life forever. If only he knew the life he'd stumbled upon….

Chapter 1

Kaedon couldn't believe his luck as he found himself within the comforts of a stranger's home with his leg elevated in a soft recliner chair dressed in a pair of fitted sweatpants and a Tweety Bird T-shirt that looked ridiculously awkward on his bulky frame. However, he was safe from the vicious storm outside and whatever else threatens to haunt his true existence.

As for the woman who rescued him, Kaedon only saw her in fleeting images as she whipped about making sure he was settled in comfortably and tending to her own personal business at hand.

But what little he did see of her, Kaedon was aware that she wasn't that much older than he was. Maybe by a few years or so. However, she was a woman of little words and a whole lot of spirit. Yet, all the reason for him to be grateful for what she had done for him. Not many women would brave a storm that fierce to go save a total stranger by any chance.

To Kaedon, this wasn't no ordinary woman. She was one worth admiring and getting to know.

And that's exactly what he planned to do. For it's not every day you stumble into the life of a woman who isn't afraid to take a risk as challenging as the one she now found herself being a part of.

Kaedon released a gentle sigh and stared at the ice pack lying across his swollen ankle.

Moments later, the woman reappeared, but this time dressed in khaki shorts and a nice fitting cotton blouse, with two coffee mugs in her hands. It was then that Kaedon really got a good look at her now that her shoulder length hair wasn't hanging loosely and wet about her face. And what a beautiful face it was. Kaedon became lost in her beauty for a moment, until she spoke up and snapped him out of his reverie.

"I'm not a coffee person," she began, offering Kaedon one of the colorful mugs. "But hot chocolate is my thing. I love making it from scratch."

"Hot chocolate is perfect," said Kaedon, taking a sip of the drink and loving its rich flavor. He then looked up at her and nodded his approval. "I've never tasted any hot chocolate this damn good."

She beamed at the compliment. "Thank you."

From where he sat in the recliner nursing his drink, Kaedon watched with intrigue as the beautiful stranger turned away from him to go take her position on the sofa chair across from him. It was hard not to watch the swing of her firm hips, and the sway of her bubble butt move gracefully with every step. She had a banging body that many women would die for. One that reminded Kaedon how lucky he was to be rescued by such a magnificent creature as she.

After taking her seat across from him, she crossed her legs ladylike and stared directly at him.

"Now," she replied. Would you mind telling me what the hell were you thinking being out there in that storm?"

"My car broke down not too far away from here and I decided to run the rest of the way."

"To where?" She asked.

He hesitated. "Just over on Hamilton Street where my sister live," said Kaedon.

"So, you thought that it was best to run the rest of the way in a rainstorm instead of calling her to come pick you up?"

"I wouldn't have called my sista to risk going out there for me?"

"Aren't you worth the risk?" She said.

"How about asking yourself that question, beautiful," Kaedon said before meeting her intense gaze. "Was I worth taking the risk of saving a complete stranger?"

For a long moment, she did not respond to his question. After about a minute she looked up at him and said, "What is your name, if you don't mind me asking?"

"Kaedon," he said. "Kaedon Smith."

She nodded. "I'm Trenika."

"Trenika." Kaedon nodded. "Cool."

"Well, Kaedon. I think it would be wise to call your sista and let her know what happened and that you are safe," Said Trenika, lifting her cup for another drink of her steaming hot chocolate.

"If I had a phone to use, I would."

"Really?" She gave him a curious glance. "In today's time, it's surprising to see someone without any form of some type of technology. You can use my phone."

Again, Kaedon watched as she rose to her pedicured feet and exited the room only to return moments later. Trenika, with her smartphone in hand, moved in his direction to offer him her phone to use.

"Thank you." Kaedon accepted the phone and wasted no time dialing out. When he didn't get an answer, he then proceeded to send out a text message.

In waiting, Trenika watched him closely and with open interest. To her, Kaedon was a mystery before her, there was something about him that hinted warning. But she cast her worries aside and focused on what matters she could control. Like keeping her distance and keep him talking, so maybe he could reveal something she could use against him in case things go left.

Trenika wasn't your average type of woman; she was used to holding her own.

"No answer again," Kaedon replied after making the call a second time.

No sooner than those words left his mouth did the downpour outside begin to fall harder against the roof overhead. It sounded like miniature stones were slamming against the roof of the house.

"Sounds like the rain isn't doing no slacking up." Kaedon broke the silence between them.

"Sounds like it," she answered with a hint of aggravation. "Look, Kaedon. I have a real problem with trusting people, especially people I don't know."

"You won't have no problem out of me, Trenika."

"Listen," she said firmly. "There will not be a problem because I have a gun, and I am licensed to carry." To confirm her statement, Trenika then materialized with what looked like a small automatic weapon. She placed the gun next to her and leaned forward to face him. "Be grateful for what I did for you and respect me and my household. Understand?" She spoke firmly.

Kaedon nodded. "Understood."

Next, Trenika rose up to her feet again and asked Kaedon to toss her the phone. He did as he was told, and she snatched the phone right out of the air. Then, with her phone and gun, Trenika disappeared back down the hallway towards the rear of the house.

Sitting there in the recliner, Kaedon removed the ice pack from his wounded ankle and reached down to massage his leg. He was just making sure if needed, that he could make a run for it if Trenika decided to get carried away with her little gun.

He hadn't underestimated her for a second, yet it was very clear she was not to be tested.

It was obvious Trenika was the truth.

And she was so beautiful.

A goddess.

A couple minutes later, Trenika returned with a fluffy pillow and a blanket in hand. She brought it over to him and Kaedon took it.

"Trenika?" Kaedon took her by the hand.

"Yes." She glared down at him.

"You can trust me, okay? I'm the least of your worries," said Kaedon

Snatching her hand away, she said. "I hear you talking. It's getting late. No one should be out there in the storm at this time. Tonight, you get some rest. But tomorrow you must leave, Kaedon."

"I gotcha," he said. "Tomorrow."

"The bathroom is down the hallway, first door on your left. Goodnight, Kaedon." Without another word, she took her leave, leaving Kaedon staring after her in silent wonder. Moments later came the sound of her bedroom door closing shut.

"Okay, Kae. You heard what she said," Kaedon muttered to himself as he spread the blanket out over him. As he settled himself in for what he figured would be a restless night, Kaedon thought back on the situation he recently left behind.

If only Trenika knew of what type of person she had welcomed into her home.

Kaedon could only hope that he gets away before she did find out the truth. Because all it takes is for her to learn who he was and what was done for him to be where he was at that very moment. Trenika would not be happy at all, not that she was at that particular moment after taken in a complete stranger.

Kaedon couldn't for the life of him take that risk of her finding out that he was a wanted man. So tomorrow, he will leave and never to return back there again.

Back in her bedroom, Trenika snuggled beneath the warmth of her comforter and dwelled on her current situation. Earlier when she was completing her task of straightening up her kitchen after fixing a light dinner, some unknown force lured her into the living room where she heard Kaedon's cry from outside within the rainstorm. When

Trenika peered through the blinds outside, there he was lying on the ground after taking a hard fall.

The rain was pouring down angrily from the murky skies as she watched Kaedon pick himself back up to his feet only to fall down again. The urge to go out there and save him was powerful, but she fought against it long enough to change her whole mindset.

Before she even realized what she was doing, Trenika had taken ahold of Kaedon and was helping him toward the safety of her home.

Since making that concrete decision, Trenika was still wrestling with her conscious wondering whether she had made the right choice or not. For all she knew, Kaedon could be a stone-cold killer. It was obvious Kaedon wasn't your ordinary black man neither. She knew a gangsta when she saw one. But for some reason Kaedon was a whole other type of gangsta and he was far from the gentle, respectful character that Kaedon presented.

But overall, he was a man, and it has been a very long time since she let another man into her world. Lord knows another man is the last thing she wanted to deal with. The last man she let into her life crushed her spirits. He had literally broken her down.

That was nearly four years ago, and she was still having side effects from the trauma he'd caused. It was the main reason why she carried a gun now, because he was still out there and probably still looking for her to claim what he feels is rightfully his.

Trenika was a good judge of character and from what she saw of Kaedon, he didn't seem like the type of man that would mistreat a woman the way her last man did. So, until he is out of her life comes tomorrow, Trenika would watch him closely and keep her guard up.

"Kaedon," she whispered softly before allowing her eyes to finally close and drift off.

Chapter 2

Kaedon too had dozed off finally, having let the melodious sounds of rain outside soothing his soul. But before he could get into the groove of a deep sleep, he was awoken by an unknown occurrence.

After two attempts to awaken him, the third attempt is what did it when he felt his nose was being pinched. Kaedon bolted up in the recliner chair, eyes wide and alert. But to his surprise, there stood a little girl in her pink pajamas grinning at him.

For a minute, Kaedon just sat there staring at the pretty little angel. He wasn't sure whether this was a dream or reality. But then the throbbing sensation from his twisted ankle was all the indication he needed to know that he was not dreaming.

Once he realized he was not dreaming, Kaedon looked about the room in search of Trenika. All he saw was a dim lit room, empty of any other presence other than his and the child's. Where was Trenika? He wondered.

"Juice?" Said the little girl, as her big round brown eyes stared up at him with innocence.

"Huh?" He replied, not sure what to do.

"I want juice," she said.

"Juice?" Kaedon said.

The child nodded eagerly and before he could decide what to do, the little girl took him by the hand and pulled.

Now was the time for Kaedon to make the smartest decision he would ever have to make in his life. To do what the child wanted and get her what she desired. Or deny her and risk her crying out and bringing Trenika in with her gun and shoot him.

"Juice, okay. I'll get you some juice, baby girl," said Kaedon once they made it into the kitchen.

"No," she said.

"No?" He looked at her. "I thought you said you wanted some juice?"

"Tiger," she said. Then, she pointed her little finger up toward the top of the fridge.

When Kaedon followed her gaze, his eyes landed on a selection of cereal lining the top of the fridge. There was a box of Lucky Charms, Fruit Loops, Coca Puffs and Frosted Flakes. It was the Frosted Flakes that she wanted, and so Kaedon retrieved them for her and prepared her meal quietly as he could.

"Aryanna?" Said Kaedon, observing the photos of the little girl plastered on the refrigerator door along with some of her and Trenika together during happy times.

"Me," Aryanna replied, pointing at herself as she watched Kaedon open the fridge to retrieve the milk. She was a sweet little thing, very determined, and to Kaedon, very manipulative as well.

After fixing her bowl of Frosted Flakes the child made a point of him making a bowl for himself. So, Kaedon did as he was told and fixed himself a bowl of cereal next.

"Eat," said the child, pointing at the chair closest to the one she was occupying.

"You are a stubborn one, aren't you, Aryanna?" Kaedon stroked her round cheek, and she blushed. "How old are you baby girl?"

After dumping a spoonful of milky cereal in her mouth, the child used both of hands to make three fingers stand out. "This many," she replied chewingly.

"Three years old?"

Aryanna nodded. "I'm three," she said.

"I can't even remember the last time I was three," Kaedon said before eating his bowl of cereal.

"How many you?" Aryanna said.

"Me?" Kaedon pointed at himself. "How old am I?"

Again, she nodded her little curly head.

Outside the kitchen doorway was Trenika, easing down the hall toward the inside. Neither one of them had a clue that their conversation had woken her up. But Trenika didn't want to interrupt their vibe just yet, she decided to see how things panned out first.

"I'm twenty-eight," said Kaedon. "That's twenty-five years older than you."

"Older than my mommy?" The little girl asked.

"I'm not sure. Maybe, maybe not. But your mommy is pretty, just like you." Kaedon brushed a finger over her little button nose and made her giggle. "One day you will grow up to be proud to have a mommy like yours, Aryanna," he told her.

"You have a mommy too?"

Kaedon shook his head. Not anymore. All I have is a big sista who thinks she's my mommy, though," he said humbly. Not in a million years would Kaedon ever guess that he would be up in the middle of the night having a conversation with a three-year-old. He was a wanted man by the cops and street goons alike, yet here he was sharing quality time with a child.

Aryanna didn't goad him on, instead she gave her bowl of Frosted Flakes her undivided attention. She was an active little sweet thing. Kaedon wondered what part her father played in her life.

"Aryanna?" Kaedon spoke up again.

"Huh?" The little girl looked up at him with tender brown eyes and milk dripping from her chin.

"Do you have a daddy?"

That's when Trenika spun into the doorway. "I don't think that's any of your business, Kaedon. Aryanna, get back to bed right now!" She said, stepping around the table to help her daughter down from the chair she was in.

The moment she laid eyes on her mother, Aryanna lost all interest in her bowl of cereal and hid her hands behind her back.

After helping Aryanna down from her chair, the girl then stepped over to hug Kaedon's leg before darting off down the hallway to her room. In the process, Trenika gave Kaedon a look that meant nothing good would come out of this.

Kaedon tossed his arms up in surrender. "I was dead sleep when she woke me up and made me fix her breakfast at 1:00 in the morning."

"You do everything a child tells you to do?"

"If they're as pretty as Aryanna." Kaedon shrugged his shoulders. "I guess so."

"You should have called for me, Kaedon."

"And risk disappointing her, then maybe gettin' shot in the process? I don't think so. I would have done anything for that little girl."

"Even jump off a cliff?" Trenika gave him a stern look before spinning on her heels to go look after her child.

With the shake of his head, Kaedon poured what was left from Aryanna's bowl into his. Then, he proceeded to polish off the bowl of cereal in silence. When Trenika finally returned to the kitchen, Kaedon was two spoonful's from done with his meal. Trenika ignored him as she replaced the milk jug back into the fridge and set the empty bowl Aryanna had used into the kitchen sink.

"She wouldn't even finish eating her supper but could eat cereal," said Trenika before snatching the bowl away from Kaedon after he tilt it towards his mouth to drank down the rest of the milk inside.

"What is your problem, Trenika?" Kaedon replied grudgingly. For a split second there, he had forgotten all about being the stranger and guest in someone else's house at the moment.

But it was too late to take it back and so Trenika gave him what he asked for.

"My problem is you, Kaedon," she said straightforwardly. "You don't just come in someone's home and take matters in your own hands when it's not yours to take. The last thing Aryanna needs is to grow attached to someone like you who won't last no more than a moment in her life. I'm not saying it's all your fault, but when it comes to someone else's child." She paused for a moment to catch her breath. "I suggest you let the parents make that decision. You should have called for me, Kaedon."

"Okay. I'm sorry. It'll never happen again," Kaedon told her in his calm collected tone.

"I know it won't, Kaedon. You're outta here tomorrow. Simple as that," she said. Trenika then turned back for the kitchen sink to rinse off the dishes that had just been used.

From where he sat at the kitchen table, Kaedon could reach out and grab ahold of her if he chose to do so. But he had no right to do such a thing, his actions would have been in total violation.

"Do you have children, Kaedon?"

"Not any that are biologically mine. My sista Ciera has two little boys and they're more like my sons they are their own biological fathers."

"How old are they?"

"Malik is six and Tyquan is four."

"And their real fathers?"

"One's in prison serving a quarter bid and the other one is too much of a Molly head to give a damn. But my sista is the best thang that could ever happen to those boys. They're smart and disciplined. What more could you ask for?" Kaedon pushed back his seat and stood up.

16

When Trenika turned around to face him, she had to look up at Kaedon. He was six foot two and solid 200 pounds. In her eyes, he was all man. But he made her a little nervous, especially with the way his deep dark brown eyes bore into hers. Trenika had to get away from him before she lost all sense of what little innocence she had left.

Of course, Kaedon read her body language and understood it quite well. But he didn't want to press his luck with Trenika, it just wouldn't be right.

"What about Aryanna?" He replied. "Is her father active in her life?"

"That's a subject I don't care to discuss with you, Kaedon. Let's not get too personal. Remember, you're just here –"

"Until tomorrow," he cut her off. "Yeah. I know. You've reminded me of it a hundred times already. But what I don't understand is this, Trenika. How come it's okay to ask me personal questions and I cannot do the same with you?" Kaedon watched as she secured the cereal box on top of the table and replaced it on the back of the fridge.

Trenika avoided eye contact with Kaedon as much as possible. She couldn't stand to face him with the truth. "Did he hurt you that bad?" He insisted.

"Kaedon, please just let it drop. There's no way you could understand the pain that man has taken me through. You have to get some rest now," she said as she neared the kitchen doorway. "You have a big day tomorrow."

With that being said, Trenika made her exit and never looked back.

"Kae, what the hell have you gotten yourself into?" Said Kaedon to himself as he limped his way back to his waiting recliner chair.

Once there, Kaedon laid his tired body down into the comfort of the chair and tossed the blanket over his body. The rain was still busy outside, but not quite as vicious as it was before. For a while, Kaedon just laid there listening to the sounds of rain slamming against the roof and the thunder growling in the distance. But neither was as intriguing as that of Trenika and her painful past.

Kaedon really wanted to know her story, to understand why she was so bitter inside.

What could have a man had possibly done for her to be so angry and hurt that she puts up a protective shield against anyone who dare to get close to her? It's situations like these that make Kaedon wants to dig deeper just to get to the root of the matter.

"Tomorrow," whispered Kaedon as sleep gradually drew him closer. "Tomorrow we'll see," he said.

Chapter 3

The next time Trenika woke up she did so to the unmistakable sound of glass breaking and Aryanna crying out for her.

"Ary!" Trenika tossed back the comforter and bolted from the bed. She hurried across the room for the door and across the hall into her daughter's bedroom. Aryanna was sitting in the middle of her princess theme bed looking for her and back to the broken bedroom window where a fallen tree branch was protruding from.

Outside the storm was raging as rain fell in thick sheets and the wind tearing up everything in its wake. From the broken window, rainwater poured inside the child's bedroom nonstop.

"What's going on?" Kaedon suddenly appeared in the bedroom doorway looking panicked. Upon seeing him, Aryanna reached out her little arms toward him and Trenika pulled her back safely against the comfort of her embrace.

Kaedon gave her a testy look before pushing past them to get to the broken window.

"Watch out for the glass, Kaedon!" Said Trenika, trying her best to stay calm amidst the storm. Without responding to her warning, Kaedon stepped over before the window to assess the damage. Then, he took ahold of the thick branch and shoved it back out through the window. Next, he began moving what precious valuables of Aryanna's things away from the water that could be damage. Such as her princess floor rug, her floor lamp, her chest full of toys and whatnots. He moved quickly and swiftly, doing everything he could to save Aryanna's kingdom. As she stood there watching him work, the look on Trenika's face was priceless. To witness him go to all the trouble to save what belonged to her daughter left her plenty of room for admiration. To her, this was something a real true father would do for her, his precious child.

"Now I gotta go patch up the window from the outside," he said minutes later.

"From outside, Kaedon? Really?" Trenika replied.

"Really. Do you have any duct tape or anything I can use against water? Anything?" When she told him there was a roll of duct tape in one of the kitchen drawers, Kaedon hurried off to go get it. Either he was too distracted to feel the pain in his swollen ankle or he just didn't give a damn about the pain. Just as long as he could do what needs to be done to save the day.

Tomorrow, thought Trenika with a grudge. What would she have done if Kaedon wasn't around? Was this some kind of sign that God was showing her to make her take things in a different perspective now? Whatever it was, Trenika was grateful to have Kaedon there or she wouldn't have known what to do if her and Aryanna had been alone.

Out the patio door Kaedon went to go patch up the broken bedroom window like he said. Meanwhile, Trenika grabbed her cellphone and headed off to the kitchen. There, she logged her phone onto YouTube where Aryanna could watch one her favorite cartoon videos. She sat her daughter down and told her to watch the video while she prepares something for them to eat. It was a little past nine o'clock in the morning and there was light outside. Not much, but enough to see what's going on.

While Aryanna slowly began to get into her cartoon video, Trenika set a few things out and headed off down the hall toward the bedroom. And to her astonishment, Kaedon already had the window blocked off with what looked like one of her thick black heavy duty Hefty trash bags. There was no further leakage of rainwater coming into the room from the broken window. Kaedon had definitely made sure of that. Sense of pride swelled up inside of her as she dwelt on the prospect of Kaedon being there for her after how harshly she treated him the night before.

"Lord, why now? Why him?" Trenika murmured to herself. Her mind was reeling in so much at one time that it made her lightheaded a little.

Suddenly, the sound of the patio door opening and closing shut brought her out of her current state. When she backed out of her daughter's bedroom, she landed in the path of Kaedon's approaching figure. Trenika felt her heart quicken at the sight of Kaedon pulling off the t-shirt she'd given him to wear. The ripples and muscles along his upper body sent chills running down her spine. Even her panties dampened a little at all the sexiness that was standing before her.

"I think it's about time for a quick shower this time, don't you agree?" Kaedon replied, flexing his bulging muscles without even trying.

"You know where the bathroom is." Trenika turned away from him quickly before the wicked thoughts got the best of her.

She was trying hard not to give in.

With that cocky grin of his, Kaedon entered the bathroom and shut the door behind him. By now, it was obvious there was a sexual attraction existent between the two. While Kaedon was patient enough to let her decide what she wanted to do, Trenika was fighting the urge not to rape him where he stood. It's been a long time since she had some dick, and Kaedon came interrupting her life is only making things worse.

Just giving her body up to him for the sake of sexual pleasure would not be that easy. Lord knows she wishes it was, but there was also so much that comes with the sexual pleasure. And that was a reality that she knew Kaedon would not settle for. Loving her came with a price that she felt no ordinary man would be willing to sacrifice their futures for. She was more than what meets the eye. The love she had to offer did not come cheap.

Instead of giving in to her sexual desires, Trenika went to go retrieve Kaedon's clothes from the dryer in the back. She folded them up and left them on the toilet seat for when he gets out of the shower. Then, back to the kitchen she goes where her daughter awaits her presence.

She needed all the distractions she could get to keep from thinking about the man in her bathroom. A gangsta who seems to know what she's thinking, but too decent of a man to embarrass her with the truth. "Oh Kaedon," she whispered. "What are you doing with me?"

When Kaedon finally exited the bathroom, he followed his nose straight to the kitchen. Inside the kitchen, Aryanna was just finishing up her jellied toast and scrambled eggs. Trenika, who stood leaning against the kitchen counter crunching on a piece of toast and staring at her daughter, looked up at his entry and smiled weakly. Without a word, she set her food aside and began preparing his plate.

"A real breakfast in the middle of a rainstorm," Kaedon replied as he took his seat next to Aryanna.

"It was worth the risk," said Trenika.

Kaedon accepted his plate of food.

"I remember when I was a little boy living with my Grandma Lillie. Whenever it would storm like this, she always unplugged everything and kept all lights off." Kaedon nodded his head when his glass of orange juice was placed on the table before him. "She would always say get y'all tails somewhere and stay put. I could never stay put. It was moments like those I'd just let my imagination run wild."

"Sounds like my Nanna Cora," said Trenika.

"Where are you originally from, Trenika? Because I've been living in this small town all my life and I've never seen your flower a day in my life."

"My flower?" She glanced down at him.

"Your beautiful face."

"I don't know about all that. But I'm originally from New Orleans, the Seventh Ward."

"And how long you've been down here?"

"About four years now," she answered softly.

"Why did you leave home to come live in a quiet small town like this?"

With the look she gave him, it was obvious that his question diseased her. So, she snatched up a dish towel and asked him to look after Aryanna while she goes tend to the mess in her bedroom. Then, she was gone, leaving Kaedon staring after her in quiet concern.

A moment later, little Aryanna abandoned her chair and was climbing up onto Kaedon's lap with her mother's cell phone in hand.

"Cartoons," she said to him, pointing a little chubby finger at the screen.

"Lemme see, baby girl," Kaedon replied the instant the house begin to shiver from the deep growl of thunder outside. Even Aryanna shivered in his lap and laid her curly head against his shoulder.

Remembering what Trenika had told him the night before about Aryanna and her needs and her being easily to grow attached. But what does it look like for him to call her when the child needs a little affection? He couldn't just tell the little girl scram.

And that today is the tomorrow that Trenika was so adamant about him remembering. Kaedon felt he wasn't going anywhere today too. The storm was still raging outside, and he didn't think Trenika had the heart to force him out there. So, the longer he remained in their company, there was a possibility that Aryanna would grow emotionally attached anyway.

But then again, he could just walk away from it all and man the storm on his own.

"Cartoons," Aryanna persisted. She gazed up at him with those big lovely brown eyes and right then, Kaedon knew he couldn't just walk away just like that.

"Okay, baby girl. I got something you'll like," said Kaedon, taking possession of the phone.

When Trenika looked in on them a minute later, she was not prepared to see what she saw.

"Kaedon," she replied with a frown. "I thought we had this talk last night about—"

"Chill out." Kaedon held up a patient finger and shook his head slowly. In his lap, Aryanna was so into the Looney Tunes cartoon he had found on YouTube that she didn't even look up. She looked so happy and comfortable that Trenika didn't want to interrupt their moment. With the roll of her eyes and the release of a frustrated breath, Trenika turned away from the scene before her and marched back up the hallway.

A smirk spread across Kaedon's face as he settled in to enjoy the cartoon as well.

Somewhere down the hall, Kaedon could hear Trenika stomping her feet as she walked banging stuff around in her attitude. She was doing it on purpose because she's in her feelings about a strange man entering her world and disturbing her order of things.

Trenika couldn't deny the fact that it was easier having a man around the house. But in her heart of hearts, she knew that man won't stick around long.

Especially when or if she decided to tell him the truth about who she was.

That he wasn't the only one running away.

She was a wanted woman, too.

Chapter 4

"Yo', Twan. What's the word?" Kaedon spoke into the receiver as he kept his tone low within the four walls of the bathroom. There was not a better time to reach out to his main man than now while Trenika was upfront sleep with her daughter.

"Bro, you scared me for a minute," came the reply from Antwan Jackson, which was someone whom Kaedon had known since they were in grade school. If there was anyone Kaedon trusted beyond measure, it was Twan, for his current predicament was evidence in itself. It was Twan who helped him escape from jail.

"Where the hell are you, bro?" Twan asked.

"I'm safe, my nigga. The storm blew me somewhere I wouldn't have imagined I'd be in million years I would be right now."

"But are you still close to reach?"

"Very," said Kaedon.

"Can I come check you out? I mean, do you need me to slide through or something?"

"Not right now, bro. I'll let you know. I'ma utilize this spot for as long as I can. But what I need you to do is be my eyes and ears for now."

"They already got Ciera's spot on lock right now. She can't even take a piss without them crackaz all up in her ass. They're monitoring her hard!"

"Shit." Kaedon dropped his head. The last thing he needed was to bring his sister any more trouble than he already has. The whole thing about him being wanted for murder was more than enough to stress about.

It was a nightmare. Literally. The way that man was killed that night was like something straight out of a horror film.

"Okay. You just make sure you're secured. By now them people are searching high and low for me."

"Not in this weather," said Twan. "You got all types of emergencies going on around here. People losing power, car accidents, trees fallin' on top of houses. They lookin', but they can't manage a manhunt in a rainstorm. So, wherever you're at that's where you need to stay put for the time being."

"Watch your back out there, Twan."

"I got this, bro."

Kaedon shook his head. "Don't let Vega get too close. Trust me, that nigga know I'm coming for him. He set me up for the kill and I can't let that slide."

"Yeah," Twan said grudgingly." That was some foul shit that nigga did."

"He's gonna get what's coming to him real soon."

"Most definitely," Twan agreed.

After sharing a few more words with his main man, Kaedon disconnected the call. Then he deleted the number and saved a short inscription in Trenika's inbox. Maybe she'll get around to reading it whenever she wasn't trying to beat him with mind games.

Or maybe until after he's gone.

When he was satisfied with what he wrote, Kaedon then rose up from the toilet seat and flushed it before making his exit.

In the living room lying on the sofa sound asleep with her daughter lying on top of her was Trenika. She looked so peaceful lying there breathing softly. So beautiful she was.

So tough and thriving. But also scared, so afraid of just letting her hair down for a change.

"Who are you, Trenika?" He murmured as he stood there gazing down upon her.

Trenika stirred in her sleep which caused Aryanna to do the same. Which was all the reason for him to reach down for the child and lift her slowly up into his arms. Automatically, Trenika's eyes fluttered opened and she sat up instantly. "What're you doing?"

"Shhh." Kaedon kissed Aryanna's cheek before placing her down onto the shorter sofa. Then, he used the blanket that he slept under the night before and laid it down over the child to keep warm.

Without a word, Trenika watched as Kaedon eased back over to where she lay on the sofa. Next, he placed a gentle hand on top of hers and told her to relax, and to lay back down. Hesitantly, Trenika did as he asked and turned her attention fully on him as he sat there with his back against the sofa.

"What is it, Kaedon?" She sensed his troubled mind.

"Life," he said. "Life in general."

"So, what is your life like?" She asked, staring at the back of his head.

"Do you really wanna know, Trenika?"

"Yes," she sighed.

"And then you tell me yours?"

No answer.

He shook his head wearily. "That's just what I thought," he replied with a light chuckle.

Still, no reply.

"Life often goes differently than we envision or desire, Trenika. I've never meet anyone whose childhood dream was to end up abandoned, abused, addicted, or go to prison over some dumb shit. Nor have I meet anyone who prayed for a pandemic, or this fuckin' rainstorm." Kaedon shrugged his shoulders, adjusting to the moment.

"I'm listening," she said.

He continued. "People don't get married hoping for a divorce. They don't have kids and dream that they'll be sick or run away from home," said Kaedon. Behind him, he heard Trenika groan in response to his words of expression. "We don't enter relationships hoping they'll end in betrayal. No, we dream of all the good shit life has to offer."

"But then," Trenika interjected, "Life happens, and we find ourselves in turbulent situations that are not always of our doing," she said.

Now it was his turn to groan, having let her words hit home in regard to his current situation. Kaedon turned around to look at her and said, "Our hearts hurt, Trenika, but we cope. We put up facades, search for muthafuckers who understand our pain, or turn to some type of distraction to numb our wounds."

"Water coloring, painting," Trenika stated.

Kaedon looked her dead in the eyes. "Gangsta shit, smoking weed, and fuckin' bad bitches," he said and got slapped in the back of the head.

"You're silly."

"But I'm graveyard serious, though."

Right then, she sat back up in the sofa and patted the cushion space next to her. "Get up here before I change my mind."

You didn't have to tell him twice. Kaedon eased up onto the sofa next to Trenika. Then she scooted over to the other end of the sofa to put space between them. They looked at each other for a long moment, then it was Kaedon who broke the connection first. Something was happening between the two of them and it was happening fast.

"Darkness can make anyone question the goodness and the presence of God," said Trenika.

"What made you say that?" He answered.

Trenika dropped her head for a moment as if trying to find the right words to say what she needed to say. As he sat there watching her, Kaedon could tell she was having conflicting thoughts on what the next words that came out of her mouth should be. The mixed emotions she was having became flashes of facial expressions as she struggled to find her words.

"Just spit it out, Trenika," he said impatiently.

"It's not that easy, Kaedon. Can't you tell? I'm really in a dark place right now." "Are you dying, Kaedon?"

"No. But –" He paused to hear her out.

"Well, I am, Kaedon. I'm dying. This beautiful flower you see right now is dying. And I can't do a damn thing about it except embrace it." Trenika had tears welling up in her eyes and it was then that Kaedon finally reached out to her.

The moment he touched her, came the startling sound of someone pounding on the front door. Immediately, Kaedon bolted to his feet and stared in the direction of the door.

"Calm down." Trenika stood and said. "That's probably Lisa coming to check up on us."

"Who is Lisa?" He asked.

"A very good friend of mine and Aryanna's godmother. Now, please humble yourself and wipe that look off your face." Just like that, Trenika was back to her old self again. The moment of truth had been broken and it was all Kaedon could think about.

Dying? What does she mean by dying? Kaedon was very disturbed by the thought of her dying. To him, she looked as healthy as an athlete. The woman was so confusing at times he didn't know what to believe. But one thing is for damn sure, though. Kaedon had gotten her to finally open up. All it took was a little more pushing. He had her.

Chapter 5

Upon her entrance, Lisa Brown was just as lively of a character as her flamboyancy. The woman had more bracelets and earrings on that Nan African goddess. Chunky and loud, but naturally beautiful in spirit and features, Lisa was one of those type who would bring life to any party and her actions spoke louder than words.

At the sound of her godmother, little Aryanna stirred awake and sat up on the sofa. She rubbed the back of her hand over her sleepy eyes and reached out to Lisa. Godmother Lisa scooped the child right up into her arms and rained kisses upon her face. "I knew calling you would be a waste time so I came over instead." Lisa looked up at Trenika and said.

"We're surviving," said Trenika. "I know that's right. I was praying you and my baby boo was all right. The storm is really messing up a lot of people's lives out there."

"How so?" Trenika reclaimed her seat on the sofa and glanced around in search of Kaedon. "Girl, on my way over I saw at least three car wrecks. A tree fell onto a powerline downtown and killin' all the power up and down Highway 90...I mean Pat Thomas! All types of shit is going down out there." Lisa bounced Aryanna on her knee as she sat across from Trenika, whom she noticed wasn't looking much like herself than usual.

"What's up sis?"

"Kay!" Aryanna was suddenly whipping her head around in search of Kaedon. "Mommy, where Kay?" she asked before telling Lisa to put her down.

"Now, what's her problem?" Lisa watched the little girl scurry away and out of her room.

Of course, Trenika knew what her problem was, but she failed to voice it right away.

"Is Mama Rose, okay? I should call her."

"Mama is good, Nika. How about you? Spill it. What's that look I'm seeing right now?"

"What look?" Trenika refused to look her way.

Lisa gave her a don't-try-me look that Trenika knew all too well.

"You've been my bitch for almost fifty damn years. You don't think I know you by now? I know when something is bothering you. What is it?"

Lisa was also stubborn too when she wanted to be. Though she had a habit of making something good out of every situation, no matter how serious it may be.

Trenika wondered what her friend's reaction would be if she found out Kaedon was inside the house.

Suddenly, Aryanna burst out laughing at something that had them both looking in its direction. The rain outside seemed to have slackened up a lot, making it clearer to hear things inside now. Especially with Aryanna, who was very animated with her verbal expressions somewhere beyond their line of vision.

"It's just one of them days, sis. I was banking on going to the art gallery today and the storm ruined all that. Then, I can't finish the piece I was doing because the storm throwed off my focus. I'm just not feeling it."

"That's when you work the best, sista girl," Lisa said. She had to remind her that it was during her troubled periods when she painted her best pieces.

"You're right," said Trenika. "As always."

"So, don't give me that damn lame excuse. Oh, and while I'm at it, sis. I'm hearing there's something about an escape over at the local jail. They're saying this guy is dangerous and so I suggest that you stay on point, you know, just in case."

"I got us, baby. You don't have to worry."

"You still got your gun? Lisa asked.

"Most certainly." Nodded Trenika.

"Then, I guess you're secured. I know you're capable of holding your own. Aryanna!?" Lisa stood up from the sofa and called out for the second time.

Trenika didn't move a muscle. A moment later, Aryanna reappeared in the living room, but this time pulling Kaedon along. When Lisa laid eyes on him, she had to do a double take. Then she looked from his humble face to Trenika's deer-in-the -headlights expression of being caught red handed. It was all Lisa could take before she had sit back down, cross her legs, hand under chin, and glaring over at her friend for an explanation on what's going on.

"I can explain," he replied.

"Shut up, Kaedon!" Lisa held her hand up to him. "No one asked you to say a damn thang, nigga."

Whoa. Now, Trenika was really taken aback by the fact the two know each other. Instead of speaking up, she gave Kaedon the same look Lisa was giving her.

"Okay, I see where this is going." Lisa uncrossed her legs and stood up. She then stepped forward and moved in between Aryanna and Kaedon. "Now you know you are dead ass wrong being here, nigga. Not only do you have Vega and his people looking for you out there, but the police too. And do you think by any chance either would spare my girl and my goddaughter if they found you here?" She demanded.

This was all the reason for Trenika to rise up now and confront the situation.

"Wait just a minute," said Trenika. "Lisa, what are you talking about? Kaedon, talk to me?"

"No, sis it's time for Kaedon to go!" Lisa argued.

"No. I need to know," Trenika responded

"Trust me, sis. Damn." Lisa was growing very agitated now.

Trenika shook her head no. She looked up at Kaedon with plea in her eyes. The same eyes that Aryanna saw him through, but Trenika's were more profound at this point. "No," said Trenika. "Not yet."

Releasing a frustrated breath was all Lisa could do to keep from really snapping. The last thing she wanted was to act out in front of the child.

By this time, Aryanna was already aware something very serious was going on. Which is why she now clung to Kaedon's leg, begging him to pick her up.

And that's why Trenika didn't want him to leave just yet. The attachment her daughter had on him now would be too much for her if Kaedon left now. At least not while she was conscious of what's going on.

That's what Trenika was afraid of and her concerns before the other two.

Kaedon lifted the child up into his arms and moved around Lisa to sit down in the recliner.

"Lisa sit down," said Trenika..

"Don't tell me what to do, Nika," she retorted but took her seat next. Then, she shot Kaedon a look so nasty he felt it in his soul. Right when he was experiencing the most peace than he had in a long time, here comes Lisa fucking everything up for him. However, since he was planning on sharing his truth Trenika earlier anyway, he thought now would be just as good a time as well.

"It's not what you think it is, Lisa," Kaedon looked over at her and said.

"I'm not the one that's needs convincing, nigga."

"Lisa." Trenika frowned at her.

Lisa said, "I'm just saying, sis. Stop trying to check me, I'm not the one that's wanted for murder."

And there you have it, Trenika's mouth dropped to the floor at the word murder. Kaedon looked at her and wished he hadn't. Now, she was afraid, and he couldn't change how she felt. Or could he?

"What is this about a murder, Kaedon? The truth," Trenika said in a firm tone.

"I haven't lied to you before." Kaedon kissed Aryanna on top of her head and shooed her over to her mother. The child went obediently, and Kaedon looked a little lonely for a brief moment.

All of a sudden, he felt trapped.

"About two weeks ago an associate of mine contacted me regarding a drug deal. I was selling heroin at the time. My associate, Nardo, said he had a buyer for some of the work I had agreed on a date and time. When the time came, the dude that he introduced me to was ready to purchase. He brought the money and all. But my sixth sense told me dude wasn't right. It felt like a setup. But before I could get the drop on both of them, my front door was kicked in."

"Sounds like bullshit to me," said Lisa. "Vega is saying you killed his brotha, nigga.

"But I didn't kill him," said Kaedon. "Niggas came to rob me and them clowns got caught in the crossfire. I got away while they died in the process."

"In your crib," Lisa added.

"Correct," Kaedon nodded. "In my crib."

"But how did you end up in jail? Why didn't you just run away to save yourself?" Trenika spoke up, sitting on the edge of her seat in suspense.

"I gave myself up to prevent them from fuckin' with my family. I know it sounds crazy, but I was under a lot of stress at the time. Making sure my family was safe and secure was all that mattered to me. I didn't want them being victims of my bullshit."

"Then, why escape from jail?"

"To prove my innocence," said Kaedon

"What innocence!" Lisa snorted.

"That Vega's responsible for having his own brotha killed. He got wind somehow and found out about Nardo working for the Feds setting niggas up. So, he decided to get rid of him and use me as the scapegoat. But I know something he doesn't think I know. I'ma hit him where it hurts the most," he said.

"And where's that?" Trenika asked.

That's when he got up and stepped before her and placed his hand over her heart.

"His heart," Kaedon whispered. "I know where his heart lies, Trenika. Once you attack a man's heart, you reveal his weakness. I know his weakness." He assured them both.

"Are you going to kill him too?" Trenika asked.

"Why kill a person who'll only self-destroy himself in the end?" He answered. "I have a plan."

"I believe you, Kaedon."

"You do?" A flicker of hope ignited him.

Trenika nodded yes.

"I think I'm gonna throw-up!" Lisa pretended to gag, being her dramatic self as usual.

Chapter 6

"So, you say you have a plan. Cool." Lisa paused to wipe the corners of her mouth with a napkin. "But does this plan consist of my sister being an accomplice?"

Kaedon was leaning back in his seat with half of his sandwich resting on a paper plate in front of him. Trenika had decided to make them all sandwiches for lunch and it turned out to be a good thing.

She gave the impression that she lived to feed those who cared to stick around.

Grandma Lillie always said the way to a man's heart is through his stomach. Now Kaedon was thinking, wondering if that statement applied to Trenika's doing.

"I have a plan for her too, but not that one though," said Kaedon, meeting the gaze of the woman he was now beginning to understand in a sense.

Trenika smiled softly and turned away from him. "Whatever, boy!" Lisa watched the silent interaction between him and her friend and warned Kaedon that if he hurt her, he would have a problem on his hands with her.

"That's the last thing I would do to her," he said. "She deserves to be happy for a change."

"And you're the remedy for her happiness?"

He shrugged. "No."

What he expected was for Trenika to look back at him with the questioning glance he'd grown accustomed to. But she didn't do such a thing, instead she exited the kitchen without a backward glance.

"She's good at running away," he acknowledged.

"It's the only way she feels safe, Kaedon," Lisa said this so softly it made Kaedon wonder if Trenika's running away affected her as much as it was beginning to affect him. "That girl has been through pure hell. All she knows is pain and agony. You have to be patient with that one."

"Love is patient," he replied.

Lisa slapped a hand against the table startling both of him and Aryanna, who was nibbling on her sandwich like a rabbit. "Don't use that word around her, Kaedon. Love is what brought her here in the first place."

"What do you mean?"

"It's not my business to tell."

"Not even a hint?"

She shook her head no. "Not at all."

Kaedon glanced toward the kitchen door expecting Trenika to step from around the corner.

"Don't drag her into the street bullshit, Kaedon. I mean it. I truly care about her a lot. If you're gonna handle your business, do it. Just handle it and leave no traces back here. Don't lead her on to something that you won't be able to honor."

"I honor everything I do, Lisa."

"Then, honor her fears. Honor her trust. If you're gonna be there for her, be there." Lisa looked up into his eyes and held his gaze. "Or you can just go now and save her the little tears she has left."

After finishing her lunch, Lisa then took her leave. To watch her go was like witnessing his chance of knowing a part of Trenika that she won't share with him personally fly out the window.

"Cartoons, Kay?" Aryanna said to him after following Kaedon to the door to let Lisa out. He turned towards the child and wondered- just for a moment- what it would be like if he was to remain in her life. Every child needs a father figure in their life. He never had one of those, he doesn't even know what it feels like to have one.

Especially for a little girl, having witnessed the emotions it took his own sister through growing up. He didn't want that for Aryanna. She was too precious.

What man in his right mind would neglect something so adoring as little Aryanna? Wondered Kaedon. But then he had to remind himself that neglect was on Trenika's part. She was the one who ran away and made Aryanna a fatherless child.

"Okay, baby girl. Let's go watch cartoons." Kaedon lifted her up into his arms and carried her away. He would have given her anything she desired.

But what he desired most at the moment was her mother. He wanted some answers and by all means she better not run away from him. Kaedon was fed up with the mind games. His heart was involved. The heart of a gangsta.

Trenika was awakened in the brightness of the strobe light caressing the images she was painting. Standing before the easel in front of her, her paintbrush moved gracefully along the paper to which she had pronounced with vivid colors. Upon her head was her favorite thinking cap, her eyes capturing the melodies of jazz music playing from her Bluetooth earphones. Trenika had taken heed to Lisa's words and found her solace within her art.

This was a passion and gift. Painting had also become her way of providing for her and her child. At first, the money wasn't a concern, but after the first year of arriving in Florida, money had become tight.

But that was before she began her research and began submitting her paintings into auction galleries. Her first submission rewarded her with two pieces sold. That was all the motivation she needed to stay afloat and not drown in her own misery. But then Lisa came along and became that sunshine Trenika needed in her life.

Lisa was surely a godsend.

She was true.

But it wasn't Lisa or her past that busied her mind and interrupted her thought process. It was Kaedon. It was the feeling that she was developing for him. A totally wounded stranger that stumbled into her life not even twenty-four hours ago. A man that knew what to do without her voicing it. A gangsta that longs for her type of love and affection. But her fear of giving in to him knowing he was only around for a short spell is what is keeping her at bay.

No matter how uncomfortable the thought is, but the fact still remains, she needed a man in her life.

There has been many that she could have chosen from since her arrival, but neither affected her as much as Kaedon has. It was a mistake to welcome him in knowing how effective it would be when Aryanna saw him. She didn't have time to really consider her options. She reacted off pure instinct and know she found herself in a situation.

If it was possible that she could rewind her life back to the moment when she saw Kaedon outside in that storm, would she have decided against it and not disrupt her quiet life alone with her daughter? Or would she have done the same exact thing and risk being hurt again by condescending to the need of having a man around?

All of a sudden, a pair of strong hands took ahold of her shoulders from behind and begin to massage and caress and relieve her of the tension that had built up. But the feeling was short lived until she felt the gentlest kiss placed on the back of her warm neck.

Trenika shuddered and spun around on her heels to face him head on.

"No", she replied. "I don't need that, Kaedon."

"What are you afraid of, Trenika? I mean you no harm," Kaedon told her in the most gentlest voice.

"That's where you're wrong at." She began and sat her paintbrush and watercolors aside. "I was hurting before you came into my life. And now that you are here, the pain has risen. I didn't ask for that Kaedon."

"But you are the one that brought me here."

She nodded. "I know. I was only doing what I could only hope someone would do for me."

"Help you?" He replied

"Yes."

"And haven't I done that for you in return?" Kaedon reached for her hand, and she pulled it away.

"You've done more than enough, Kaedon. I can't afford to have you here any longer or risk of Aryanna becoming dependent on you and growing so attached to the point it would destroy her in the process when it's time for you to go. I can't do this, Kaedon. I'm sorry. But you have to leave now. You'll just have to man up and weather the storm on your own."

"What if I don't want to leave?"

"You have no choice. This is my damn house."

He didn't even flinch. "And if I come back?" Kaedon was not going to make this easy for her.

"You wouldn't have no reason to come back."

"I can count several of them, Trenika."

Trenika braced herself. "This is not what you want, Kaedon. I'm dying. The man I used to love and worshipped the ground he walked on is to blame for my fears and my pain. The same man that I bought a ring for and got on one knee to propose my life in marriage. And do you know what he gave me in return?"

"What?" Kaedon sighed deeply.

Tears brimmed the rim of her eyes now. "H.I.V. The man that I dedicated my heart and my life to spoiled me and my daughter's life with H.I.V., Kaedon. So please," Trenika cried. "Please just forget about our lives, because it's not what you want. We are no good for you."

"Trenika..." He reached out.

"Go! Leave me alone!" She shoved him so hard in the chest that Kaedon nearly fell over.

"Really?" Kaedon replied. This left him baffled.

"Don't make me go get my gun," she warned, tears falling from her eyes nonstop.

For a long time, Kaedon just looked at her as though he couldn't believe how things had suddenly taken a drastic turn. He literally looked hurt over it. Then, without a word further, Kaedon turned and walked away.

He was gone.

And a piece of her heart left with him.

It was painful.

Chapter 7

The rain had its momentum for two straight days before the dark clouds broke away and allowed the sun to make its presence known. It was like a breath of fresh air to know that the storm had passed.

However, not so much with Kaedon, who for the past two days since walking out on Trenika and Aryanna was experiencing a separate storm of his own. An emotional one that has been the focal point of his sleeplessness and the reason he wasn't as focused as he should be.

H.I.V. she had said. That was a matter Kaedon had always prided himself on with dealing with women. He had always believed in practicing safe sex. He never left home without protection of some kind.

But to hear that her and Aryanna was contracted with the virus was a vicious blow to his chest. Of course, he was aware of how dirty and unapologetic women could get when they want what they want. They had a habit of saying anything that comes to mind-no matter how dumb or vulgar it sounds-to make a man lose interest in them if they're not into him.

What Trenika had professed to him two days ago wasn't just a blow-off. What she said was real. The truth of her pain had resounded in her eyes. There was no way anyone could act that damn good.

Trenika was dying. She was ruined. She was scared. More so for her child than herself. And Aryanna had no clue how deep her life was. It was a wonder her future would be like when she do become aware of her sickness and how it would affect others.

Kaedon was not prepared for that.

It was just so wrong.

If only he could find the man who destroyed their lives.

Kaedon wouldn't hesitate killing and making him pay for all the heartache and pain he cause Trenika and his beautiful little girl.

It was decided. Kaedon would find him and destroy him. He doesn't even deserve to live. That's if no one hasn't already killed him by now. But Kaedon was going to find out himself, and the man better hope he doesn't find him. Because his death was gonna be a very slow one indeed.

What he did was wrong.

Which means he had to have passed the virus to Trenika before her pregnancy or during it for Aryanna to be born with it as well.

If memory served him right, Aryanna was three years old, and she was born away from New Orleans, which she was first conceived. With Trenika having been living in Quincy for nearly four years, therefore she had learned of the virus during the middle of her pregnancy. It had to be somewhere around that time, however, the damage could not be undone.

What's a man to do for a woman and her child whose life has been compromised by a deadly disease at the risk of them not living a full healthy life?

That's the question Kaedon has been asking himself for the past two days now.

There will always be unhappiness, the reality of their situations couldn't be overlooked without consequence. What man in his right mind would subject himself to such reality as that?

It was a hard pill to swallow.

Kaedon couldn't do it.

He just couldn't.

It was insane just considering it.

Later that evening after no contact with Twan, they finally met up and got right into the first

phrase of the plan. Which was to get Kaedon's stash spot location and obtain his bank.

"I don't know why you didn't just have me get the shit for you, bro," said Twan, sitting behind the wheel of a stolen Chevy Trailblazer.

"You must think I'm stupid."

"Twan chuckled. "Ohh. You don't trust me now?"

"The way you be lettin' Sonya break your pockets with her trifling ass, you might try to use my shit to keep her from peeling your shit."

This made Twan laugh as he passed over the blunt of sour Kush they were smoking. Kaedon took the blunt he had rolled and pulled in weed smoke, exhaling long and enjoying the effects.

A nice fat blunt was just what Kaedon needed to ease his troubled mind.

Trenika's situation had thrown him all off balance. He just needed to forget about the whole thing.

"A'ight. Here we go, bro. You know the move," said Twan once he brought the vehicle to a halt outside a Pepper Hill community residence.

This was the location. Kaedon inhaled deeply, released, and exited the vehicle enroute to the front door of the gated residence. The house was of an old red brick structure with a big pecan tree taking up most of the front lawn. It was a sanctuary of Kaedon's when the streets got too tiring, and his own home didn't feel safe at times.

This was his secret hideaway.

Kaedon knocked on the front door and waited. He checked the time on his G-Shock and saw it was 8:21 p.m. Still early for old man Jake to be up puffing on his expensive pipe watching TV. From outside it appeared as though the house was dark within. But that was only because Jake preferred for his windows to be heavily curtained and shaded to keep any potential peepers from looking in.

After a few moments, Kaedon gave the door a firmer knock to rouse the old man inside.

"That's a good way to get shot, bangin' on my door like you the police, son," said Jake the instant he opened the door and saw Kaedon on his doorstep.

"You love me too much to shoot me, old man." Kaedon patted his potbelly and stepped inside.

"I got your old man hangin', boy!" Jake retorted and shut the door behind him.

"Been out of commission for a coupla weeks, but I'm back now. I got some serious business I need to take care of, and I need to hit the stash." Kaedon didn't wait for a reply and hurried down the dark hallway toward the back of the house.

"It's your business and your belongings. You don't owe me no explanation, son. But don't just come bustin' in here after being gone for so long and not ask me how the hell am I doing."

"How you doing Jake?" shouted Kaedon from the back.

"Just fuckin' peachy, son."

Kaedon laughed.

The stash spot, at the rear of the house, was in the den area behind the eight-foot bookshelf. It didn't take Kaedon long at all to retrieve the duffel bag which was his stash. He wasn't worried about it being tampered with because one thing he was sure of, and that's being Jake's respect that he had for him. Plus, the old man wasn't hard off for money. He was a retired war veteran and one helluva investor of his pension and side hustles. It wouldn't surprise Kaedon if Jake was sitting on a few million of his own.

When Kaedon returned back to the front of the house, he found the old man sitting in his favorite rocking chair. He was puffing on his favorite pipe and watching WWE Raw on TV.

"Thomas Bradwell," said Jake absentmindedly.

"Huh?" Kaedon paused.

"The boy they're saying you killed over yonder. That's his granddaddy. I know Thomas very well. If all else fails, I know where I can go to get justice for my boy. Remember, I still owe you my life after what you did for me." Jake never took his eyes off the TV screen as he said those words.

How could Kaedon ever forget that fateful morning. The old man had just gotten back in town from his fishing trip over at Lake Jackson. Jake had had a heart attack behind the wheel of his truck and crashed it into a nearby ditch. Kaedon, being the quick thinker that he was, pulled the old man from the wreckage. He loaded him into his own car and drove him to the Emergency Room. He had saved Jake's life that day. That was almost ten years ago, and Kaedon remembered it like it was on yesterday.

"I know what to do, Jake," he assured him.

"I know, son. You always do."

Kaedon then stepped over and kissed the top of the old man's salt-n-pepper head and left.

Jake was as close as a father figure to Kaedon than anyone has ever been. It was from him that he was taught the true values of responsibility. He wished the old man could live forever, but Kaedon knew that wasn't possible. Which is why he made a mental note to stay sharp and focused so that he could get back to Jake before his time finally does run out.

Back in the vehicle with his main man again, Kaedon's whole demeanor had changed.

"We good, bro?" Twan asked. "You seemed stressed."

Kaedon nodded solemnly. "I'm good. Let's go. We got some bodies to bury."

"Say no more, my nigga." Twan punched it and just like that, they were back at it again. But this time the game has changed.

The stakes were way too high.

It was war.

Chapter 8

It was a Wednesday afternoon when Trenika pulled up in the driveway of her home after running a few errands in town. Lisa was also accompanying her as well, counting down the time when they could go retrieve Aryanna from daycare. Trenika had decided to try something new out and it turns out that Aryanna was loving daycare.

To deny her daughter an opportunity to make friends and have a normal childhood was wrong in all aspects. Every child deserves to be free to grow. Especially after Kaedon had walked out on them several days ago. It brought Aryanna a sadness that burned inside every time Trenika watched her daughter wake up in search of a man that wasn't there. At times, she would call for Kaedon only to get no answer. Then, she would just crawl up into mother's lap and cry. It was heartbreaking to watch. So, for three days now, Aryanna has been slowly regaining her spirits back over at the daycare center. She now had children her age could play with. It was the perfect distraction from her worrying over Kaedon.

For Trenika as well, because the more she witnessed her daughter's sadness, it reminded her of Kaedon. She was trying to forget that he ever existed.

Yeah, right.

"Girl, where the hell are you going?" Lisa called out to Trenika. "I'm not carrying all these bags by myself."

"I'm just going to check the mail, sis," Trenika shouted back as she hurried over to the mailbox. Lisa, stubborn as she wannabe, still managed to receive all 6 bags of groceries and such. Never was she the type to back down from a challenge.

Standing next to the mailbox at the curb, Trenika opened its flap to check inside. Not much was there. She extracted all that was there and automatically began sifting through the several pieces she did have.

"What is this?" Trenika eyed the colorful greeting card envelope and wondered where it came from. It didn't have a return address which made it suspicious.

"Um, sista girl! Can I get some damn help here!" Said Lisa, using one of her thick hips to shut the back passenger door. Her arms were loaded with shopping bags, and she appeared to be struggling.

Another brief glance at the rosy- red card envelope, then Trenika went to relieve her friend from some of the shopping bags. Together, they carried the bags inside and deposited them into the kitchen. From the distance it took to move the bags from the car to the kitchen was enough to warrant Lisa a glass of water.

"Whew! Now that was a mission," Lisa said as she held the cool glass up against her forehead.

"You are so damn dramatic, girl."

"What?" Lisa downed the rest of the water and slid onto one of the cushioned bar stools before the kitchen counter.

"That wasn't no work at all," said Trenika.

"It was to me, sis."

Trenika just shook her head. "All the reason for us to start back going to the gym. We haven't been back since the pandemic hit US," she said.

"We will soon. One of these days."

"Whatever."

The doorbell rang. Somebody had come to pay a visit and Trenika wondered who it was. She went to answer the door. A fleeting thought warned her that there's a possibility that it could be Kaedon. By all means, he did say he would come back. Trenika didn't know whether to get her hopes up about that or beware of the emotional rollercoaster it could create. Trenika hoped it wasn't him.

Once at the front door, she opened it and to her surprise, it wasn't Kaedon. But the man standing on her doorstep was much older and sharp looking. He had a toolbelt and a hard hat.

"Can I help you, sir?" She asked.

"I'm here to fix your broken window. I was summoned to this address to get the job done."

Trenika found that very strange. "Um, I didn't hire your service to fix my window. May I ask who's responsible for sending you here for this job?"

For a moment, the man whose nametag read Larry lifted his clipboard to answer her question. "It only says the letter K and the job has already been paid in full. However, I would like to get out your way and get started if you don't mind," he said respectfully.

"I don't mind," she answered. "Come inside and lemme show you the damage.

"Thank you," he entered the house.

"Did the storm ever hit as hard as it did just recently?" Trenika asked.

"Ma'am. I'm a Georgia boy. I've only been around these parts a little over a year. But I'm quite sure it's had its share of rough ones," said Larry.

After showing the man the damage and leaving him to his work, Trenika returned back to the kitchen where she found Lisa fanning with the red card envelope. The look on her face was knowingly curious.

"Lemme guess. It's Kaedon," she said.

Trenika shrugged and snatched the envelope away from her friend. "I don't know yet. I haven't even opened it yet, sis," she told her.

"I'm talking about him out yonder, girl."

"Oh. That's all Kaedon's doing." frowned Trenika wishing for Kaedon to just leave her alone. She had been doing good pushing him out of her system.

When the envelope was opened, Trenika pulled free the greeting card inside. She opened the card and began to read the message within.

"Oh no!" Trenika dropped the card instantly and backed away from it as if it was a coiled rattlesnake. She looked suddenly petrified for some reason.

Seeing the dreaded look on her friend's face made Lisa climb down from the stool. She approached Trenika and took her by the arms. "Sis, what's wrong?"

Trenika was so scared she was shaking. She stared down at the fallen card and mumbled something that was so low that it was difficult to catch. Lisa released her and knelt down to retrieve the card from the floor. Trenika wrapped her arms around herself as though she had become chilled.

"You can run but you can't hide. I see you. I'm coming for what's mines," Lisa read the words that was written in bold red letters upon the card. "It was signed, Mr. November," she added.

Trenika groaned in displeasure.

"Sista girl, who the hell is this fool?" Lisa demanded, not liking what she was seeing.

"It's Romell."

"Romell?" Lisa looked shocked at this new revelation. "But I thought he didn't know where you was?"

"He obviously does now."

"But how?"

"I don't know. And I'm not taking no chances. I gotta go get Ary!" Trenika said and dashed for her bedroom to get her gun. From there, she headed straight for her car outside without waiting up for Lisa.

Reaching her daughter before it's too late was top priority.

She was frightened.

It was over.

Her worst nightmare had just come true.

"There he go right there." Twan nodded in the direction of these three guys exiting from the poolhall downtown up on The Block.

This was one of the main hangout spots in town where you're liable to meet anybody and everybody one chooses to acquaint themselves with. The Block consisted of a small juke joint of a bar, barbershop, liquor store, and just up the street was the Quincy Police Dept. The historical courthouse and neighboring shopping centers also were part of The Block.

It was your typical small town busy locations bunched all up onto one block.

"I see him," Kaedon replied.

"What the plan?"

Reaching for the 9.mm Beretta sitting in his lap, Kaedon watched as Lonzo and his two companions load up into a shiny black Range Rover. "Follow them," he said.

"Let's do it," said Twan.

If Kaedon had told him from the beginning whom he suspected, Twan would have gotten him by now. But Kaedon wanted to make sure that he was present while it went down. He would have never sent his main man on a mission alone. The mark in question was Lonzo Dennis, the first cousin of Vega, and his righthand man.

Apparently, Vega didn't have the guts to kill his own brother, so who did he trust enough to see that the deed gets done than his most trusted partner? Lonzo. Nando had become careless with his dealings with the Feds setting niggas up. Apparently, Vega was confronted about his brother's actions by some of the big dawgs and given and ultimatum. Deal with his brother personally or they would do it for him.

Respecting the game for what it was, Vega agreed to take his own flesh and blood out the game. Or else be blackballed in the street game from all major players or perhaps get the same treatment as his brother.

And Kaedon knew what he saw that evening. It was clear as rain on the back of his hand. The same hand he used to pull the trigger to kill Nardo. And no one else in area, or surrounding areas had the tattoo of a viper snake on the back of their right hand but Lonzo himself. Kaedon would bet his bottom dollar on that it was Lonzo who tried to set him up. And it was Lonzo that Kaedon planned to make him confess to his sins.

"Don't get too close, nigga. Pull back some," said Kaedon.

"I got this shit right here, bro. Chill," Twan told him as he widened the distance between them and the black SUV up ahead. "I got this under control."

Vengeance was about to be served, and Kaedon could taste it at the tip of his tongue.

The buzzing in Twan's front pocket indicated that he had an incoming call. He reached inside his pocket and sent the caller straight to voicemail. Afterward, he tossed the phone onto his lap next to the mini .14 machine gun. Twan had no time for conversation right now.

A minute later, the buzzing sound from the ringing phone against the weapon became an annoyance.

"It's Sonya," said Kaedon.

"Shit." Twan snatched it up immediately.

With the shake of his head, Kaedon knew he wouldn't just sit there and ignore Sonya's calling.

"Yeah. Bro right on deck with me right now. What's going on? Okay! Here he go. Damn!" Twan said into the phone and extended it toward his main man.

"What?" Kaedon gave him an odd look. "No!"

"Just take the fuckin' phone bro!"

Reluctantly, Kaedon snatched the phone from him and put it to his ear. "What Sonya!"

"This isn't Sonya. It's Lisa," came the reply and at the seriousness he heard in her tone, Kaedon sat upright in his seat with alert.

"What's up, Lisa?" He said evenly.

"It's about Nika," she stressed to him. "She's in trouble."

And that was all Kaedon needed to hear before everything suddenly went left.

Chapter 9

When she turned into the entrance of Little Kingdoms Daycare Center, Trenika swung her car into a parking space out front and hopped out. She was so focused on getting her daughter that she left the car on and the driver's door wide open.

Trenika entered the building like a mad woman, looking for her child around every corner. When one of the caregivers approached her, concerned about the frantic actions, Trenika expressed to the woman there has been a family emergency and she wanted her daughter.

"And whom might that be?" Asked the white woman.

"Aryanna," said one of the younger caregivers who suddenly appeared out of nowhere. "I'll go retrieve her for you," she told Trenika who only just nodded in response.

"Is everything alright, ma'am? You look a bit pale. Should I fetch the inhouse nurse for you?"

"No," Trenika said flatly.

"I'm only concerned about your health and the well-being of the children here, ma'am," said the older woman.

Trenika shrugged. "That's nice to know. I just want my daughter and nothing else."

"Suit yourself."

Minutes later, Trenika was strapping Aryanna down in her car seat and then, after all this time, she just realized Lisa was not with her. She had left her back at the house during her rush to get Aryanna. That proves when it comes down to your child, nothing else in the world matters.

Back in traffic, Trenika fished out her phone and sent a call through to her friend. Lisa was probably pissed with her for leaving her behind. Lisa answered on the first ring.

"I knew your tired ass would call me eventually. Where are you?"

"Listen to me, Lisa," Trenika cut her off. "Are you still at the house?"

"Where the hell else am I gonna go without a car? Did you get my baby boo, yet?"

"Yeah. Look. There's a black case in the closet of the art room. Secure all my completed paintings inside that black case. You'll see the wooden case for the easel in there as well. Then go into my room and pull out those two big bags beneath the bed. And my Bible. And please don't forget about Ary's favorite Tweety Bird comforter." Trenika requested this all-in-one breath.

"Are you leaving me?" Lisa sounded very depressed all of a sudden and Trenika hated it.

"I can't stay there, Lisa. It's no longer fuckin' safe for Ary and I. There's no tellin' what Romell has up his sleeve now that he knows.

"But where are you gonna go, sis?"

"I don't know. Anywhere but there. I'll know when we get to that point. Just have everything ready by the time I get there. I love you."

Lisa cried. "I love you too, Nika."

When she finally disconnected with her girl, Trenika swiped at the tears spilling from her own eyes. She didn't want to leave her friend, but the pressure was on. To ask Lisa to drop everything and come with her would be asking for too much. Lisa had her own life, her own problems, and Trenika didn't want her to abandon those responsibilities. Not like she had. Trenika had left her brother and grandmother behind in New Orleans. Including all her good childhood friends and other worldly belongings. She had run away from it all and never looked back. Romell had been the cause of that happening. He had become her real-life boogeyman.

Now, he was back for blood., Or whatever it is that he felt was rightfully his.

This time Trenika would kill him if he ever came near her or her daughter. This time she would send him running for his life for a change.

There was enough malice in her heart to do so.

Trenika was fed up.

The only reason she called Kaedon was because she believed he would do the right thing. Regardless of the differences he and Trenika had, he would not stand for what she hoped Romell wouldn't do. And besides, Kaedon seemed to be the best candidate to put up with Trenika's shit. And she wouldn't let no other man get as close to her than she already had allowed Kaedon to.

Lisa knew without a shadow of a doubt her friend felt something for Kaedon. It takes a woman to understand the virtues of another woman. But this wasn't just no other woman, this was her friend. So, if Lisa felt there was a possibility that anyone could be worth Trenika's while at this dire moment, it would be Kaedon. And just like Lisa knows her friend would, Trenika would eventually bow down to him and let him run the show.

It was best to leave it in a gangsta's hands to get the job done accordingly.

Gangstas makes the world go round.

Kaedon was her man.

Behind her the front door opened and there stood Kaedon, two big duffel bags in each hand.

"Wanna know what I was just thinking, homeboy?" Said Lisa, looking back over her shoulder at him from her sitting position on the porch steps.

"What?" He asked.

"That God doesn't make mistakes," she said. "It was pure destined that you fell in her path that day. Who knows how she would handle this situation if you hadn't come into her life?"

"She hasn't given me the pass yet."

"It's yours. Homeboy. Own it. What you do from now determines where your integrity lies."

Kaedon didn't answer, instead he eased by her with the two bags and sat them down on the ground near the bottom porch step.

When he got that call from Lisa, he dropped everything he was doing to get there. Twan was there too, pissed off at him for aborting the mission. Parked at the curb behind the window company truck was Twan, still sulking over his main man's audacity to rescue a woman he did not even know.

However, he was all for it, just as long as Kaedon didn't get too sidetracked and forget that his life and freedom was still on the line.

"There she goes," Lisa acknowledged when she saw Trenika's car drive up.

And it came to a sudden halt at the very entry of the driveway. From where he stood before the house gazing towards the car, Trenika eyed him with a tidal wave of emotions conflicting her senses. It was almost like a Mexican standoff of some sort, one waiting on the other to make the first move.

"Okay." Kaedon sighed. "Here we go!"

Taking possession of both of the big bags again, Kaedon begin carrying them toward the car. With every step he took, he never took his eyes off Trenika. And that was a mistake because he never saw the car easing up the street with an armed goon hanging out of the passenger window. It wasn't until the first-round rang out did Kaedon look in its direction.

Suddenly, automatic rounds rang out as Kaedon dropped the bags and drew his Beretta. He returned fire but moved in the opposite direction from Trenika's car. If only he could make the shooter focus solely on his target, then maybe he could prevent Trenika and her child from getting harmed in the process.

Instinct brought Twan up out of his car with his own weapon and shooting back at the enemy. But the showdown was over before it even begun. The drive-by car took its share of rounds and so did Kaedon, who fell down on one knee reaching for his chest. Then, he fell over onto the ground still clutching his gun tightly in his grasp.

"Kaedon!" Trenika panicked and called out to him.

Before darkness swallowed him whole. Kaedon lay there watching dreamily as Trenika left the safety of her car and was rushing towards him. Just like she had done when he first laid eyes on her.

"Don't leave me," he said. And that was the last words he spoke before he lost consciousness.

Chapter 10

When Kaedon eventually came to, he did so with a painful groan that made him cough harshly. Then, he sat up and looked cautiously around him. When his gaze landed on the stern mask which was old man Jake's face, he groaned again and laid back down. He wasn't dead. Kaedon, with his eyes still closed again, felt along his chest and winced loudly.

"Two solid hits to the chest is a for sure kill, son," Jake replied with a grunt. "Good thing you was wearing a vest or else I woulda been one mad coon."

The bulletproof vest. Kaedon thought as he breathed in deeply, embracing the pain in his chest. It was a damn good thing he had on that vest.

Sitting back up again from the makeshift pallet he was lying on, Kaedon surveyed his surroundings again and saw no one else in the room.

"She's okay, son. I've settled her and her youngin in your room for now. I must tell ya' boy, you damn sure got your hands full with that one." Jake chuckled and offered to help Kaedon up to his feet. The old man steadied him on his feet, looked him up and down, then clapped him in the back and told him he'd live.

"I need some water," said Kaedon.

"I'll get it," came the reply from Trenika who appeared in the doorway. She then disappeared from sight to go make sure Kaedon quenched his thirst.

Kaedon perched on an arm of the sofa chair and looked down at the two-widening bruises upon his chest. He couldn't wait to kiss his bulletproof vest for saving his life.

"A few painkillers and you're back in the groove," Jake said to him before retiring to his room.

Trenika came in next, and fed him two pills and a glass of water. She stood there watching him in silence, her questioning eyes wide with wonder and relief.

"Some more?" She asked.

With the grace of a patient man., Kaedon sat the glass down and pulled her to him. He wrapped his arms around her waist and placed his head upon chest. Not sure what to do, Trenika wrapped her arms around his neck.

"Did she see what happened?" He asked.

"Yes," she whispered.

"How is she?"

"Asleep." Trenika sighed and stroked the top of his wavy head ever so softly. "She cried herself to sleep after calling for Kae," she said. "All she kept saying, Mommy I want Kae."

A brief silence ensued between them.

"What are we gonna do, Kaedon?" She spoke up again.

Unwrapping her arms from around her waist, he stood up and took her hand. Kaedon moved over to sit down on the sofa and sat her down next to him. Again, silence filled the room around them. They looked into one another's eyes and a whole nother form of communication transpired between them. No words needed to be spoken when it was clear in their eyes what they wanted.

"I'm scared, Kaedon."

"I'm here for you," he said.

She shook her head. "I mean I'm scared of you. I'm afraid I won't be able to complete you like a woman should. You know my truth. I'll only be a burden on you."

"Do you believe in love at first sight, Trenika?" He asked, and Trenika gasped. When she rose up to leave, Kaedon grabbed her and pulled her back down. "All that running shit is over with."

"Please Kaedon. I'm hurting," she sobbed.

"Then we'll hurt together." He kissed her teary eyes and held on to her tight. "I deserve you, baby. And you're just right for me. We'll make it work. All you gotta do is trust and believe. Okay. Will you at least do that for me?"

Trenika had no words to give him, only her tears and her pain. But he didn't let go, he held on for dear life. He was scared too, but Kaedon wasn't no fool; he knew the best love a man could find was there in his arms. He would make her his if it's the last thing he does.

At nightfall, Twan pulled up to the house and honked the horn twice. The front door opened, and Kaedon hurried out to the car. After what happened today it was time to turn it up a notch and put an end to the situation. Kaedon slid onto the passenger seat and Twan offered him the blunt. He shook his head no and told him that he wanted to go in with a clear head. This was the first time Kaedon ever denied him a smoke session, which only meant to Twan that his main man was on some other shit. It was time for that gangsta ride.

Once they were in traffic, Twan put in a call to Lisa to see whether she was still on point or not. When she confirmed that Lonzo was up in his baby momma's spot still, it was all the information Twan needed to get there and get it done.

"How did you pull that off, bro?" Kaedon stated.

"Pull what off?" Twan asked.

"Lisa. So, you got her down with the lick?"

Twan shrugged behind the wheel. "She basically put herself down with the lick. Homegirl say she wants this shit dealt with immediately, so you could focus the rest of your attention—"

"On Trenika and baby girl."

"Correct."

"I admire her loyalty for Trenika," said Kaedon. He thought about Trenika and how much she was beginning to mean to him now that they were on the same page.

"What's to be admired is you, bro. Are you sure you really wanna take that route?"

"What route, Twan?"

"You know exactly what I mean, bro. When you was laid out back there earlier, Trenika told me everything. But you know where my concern lies, my nigga."

"Twan?"

"Yeah," he looked at him.

Kaedon said, "God don't make no mistakes."

"Say less, my nigga. Say less."

That was the end of that conversation for now. When they were a block away from the location, Twan made another call to Lisa for confirmation.

"The nigga is feeding his face right now. I'm looking right at him," Lisa assured him.

"Stand down, homegirl. We about to come in." Twan parked the car down the street from where Lonzo was occupying the home of his baby momma.

In the passenger seat, Kaedon thumped his fist against the chest of the bulletproof vest that saved his life only just a few hours ago. Strapped with two semiautomatic weapons, now he was ready to get shit cracking. The way he felt at that moment everybody in the house could get it.

"No kids. Okay?" It was like Twan had read his mind.

"Nigga are you ready!" Kaedon retorted.

When Twan gave the nod, Kaedon bolted from the car and made his way onto the sidewalk leading up to the designated location of the house. From somewhere in the shadows, Lisa was watching their every move. This was as far as her participation went. Her job was to keep her eyes open.

After clearing the distance to the house, Kaedon gave the hand signal and Twan nodded. Then at once they charged toward the house as Kaedon burst through the front door with one vicious kick. Twan entered the house afterwards and rushed the first person who made the wrong move.

"Surprise muthafucker!" Kaedon sneered.

"What the fuck is this?" Lonzo shot up to his feet from the plush couch he was sitting on, eating a plate of ribs and baked beans.

Kaedon rushed him next and went upside his head with his pistol. Lonzo's older son jumped up and got slapped down. While Twan had his assault rifle trained on Lonzo's baby momma and his two sons, Kaedon was wearing him out pistol whipping him something viciously.

"Now this is how we're gonna do this shit," said Kaedon once he had tired himself out of beating Lonzo.

That's when Twan tossed over the smartphone as his main man stood over Lonzo with his pistol aimed at his ugly face. It was confession time.

"Did you or did you not kill Bernard Bradwell on the day of February tenth?" Kaedon questioned him.

Lonzo didn't say a word.

When Twan grabbed ahold of Lonzo's youngest son and put the gun to his head, Lonzo got his mind right very quickly.

"I thought you'll see it my way."

"Yeah. I did it! I killed him," admitted Lonzo.

Kaedon smirked. "And who ordered you to kill Bernard Bradwell on the day of February tenth?"

For a long moment Lonzo stared blankly into space as the realization of what he was about to do would change everything. Then, after realizing the damage was already done, he gave Kaedon what he wanted.

"It was Elijah Bradwell. Vega," he said.

And that was just the tip of the iceberg. It's what would happen to Lonzo next is what made him guilty. But Kaedon got his confession, on top of every juicy detail Lonzo provided that would without a shadow of doubt sink Vega's whole ship. That same night Lonzo, shot himself in the head. He was a dead man anyway. But his death would always be remembered.

63

Chapter 11

All night, Trenika stayed up waiting on Kaedon to return. He never did return, but he called to reassure her that he was alright. Before sleep finally came, Trenika dwelled on the possibility of their relationship and would his being out all night long become a regular thing. Trenika could only pray that things would work; because she knew how deep her love can get and what it takes to complete her man. She was far from new to this.

All she knew is to love, honor, and respect her man to the point it would leave him no room for doubt. The following morning when Trenika finally woke up, she woke up to Kaedon burying his face between her legs. His lips, tongue, his oral exploration must have begun way before she woke up because her juices were running.

"Oh Kaedon," she tensed with a whisper.

Afraid she would try to run away from him, Kaedon hooked an arm around her thigh as his other arm slithered up her shirt to play with her nipples. Trenika didn't attempt to run; she gave in to the sexual pleasures he was creating. With slow gentle licks of her clitoris, Kaedon was taking her to heights she hadn't reached in years. He was taking his precious time eating her pussy as though it was his last meal. And then it happened, her flood gates opened, and Trenika's climaxing came in waves of pleasure and satisfaction. Her womb opened up to him and she just kept on coming and coming like she never came before.

When Kaedon was satisfied that he had passed the first course of action, he climbed up over her sexy body while removing her shirt in the process.

"Do I make you feel good, Trenika?"

"Yes, you do," she murmured.

Staring down into her beautiful eyes, Kaedon said, "I just need you to trust me."

"I do," she said.

And in one long stroke, he entered her paradise and Trenika screamed in pleasure, digging her nails into his back as he begin sawing in and out of her.

"Stop, Kaedon. Don't do this...please!" She cried.

"Trust me, baby."

"Kaedon..."

He drove himself deeper into her love and Trenika only thought he was not going to stop. This man had to love her to be doing this. Why was he risking it all for her if he didn't love her? As he made sweet love to her, Trenika just submitted herself to him and let him have his way.

"Don't ever stop loving me, Kaedon," she cried as he continued to long stroke her. "I need you."

"I need you too," he said.

She closed her eyes for a moment, but Kaedon demanded that she open them and look at him.

"You are so beautiful," he smiled.

"I'm coming again," she said.

Trenika then began to meet him stroke for stroke. That was all the encouragement he needed to pick up the pace. Kaedon hooked his arms underneath the back of her shoulders, found his grip, leaned in, and began to pound every inch of him into her. Again, Trenika sang her pleasure as she came, and he too released his essence in thick powerful spurts into the Trojan condom he was wearing. Trenika sighed in pure ecstasy. She was spent.

"You was wearing a condom." Trenika noticed when he finally pulled out of her.

"I told you to trust me," Kaedon replied before gathering her into his arms.

"You don't wanna hear what I had thought."

He kissed her bare shoulder.

"I know exactly what you had thought," he said.

"Kae, I want you to promise me something. Promise me you wouldn't go unprotected with me to try and prove a point. Your health is important to me too. I don't want you doing something you'll later regret," she explained to him the importance of his right to continue to practice safe sex.

"I know what I'm doing, Trenika," said Kaedon.

"Promise me, Kae!" She insisted. "Please."

"No. I don't make promises."

"Not even for me?"

This time it was Kaedon who ran away. He got up from the bed and stepped into his boxers.

"So, you're gonna just walk away when I'm trying to have a conversation with you?" She argued.

Kaedon gave her a meaningful look.

"If that's what you call a conversation by trying to force me to do something I don't do then you need to go define the real true meaning," Kaedon said and left the room and slamming the door behind him.

He didn't look back. With him doing that really had Trenika in her feelings. Now she was stuck questioning her own perspectives. Because the last thing she wanted was to run Kaedon away again, not now after she has convinced herself that he was the only man for her.

"Girl, just let that man do him," Trenika told herself.

That's what Lisa would have said. So that was that. Let her man play his position. Kaedon knows best.

When she showered and got dressed for the day, Trenika went in search of her daughter. She had heard Aryanna earlier talking and fussing about with old man Jake. By now, she probably has run the man up the wall, so Trenika thought it would be best to go save him.

Trenika wondered why the house was so quiet. After checking up front in the living room and finding it empty, she peered out the front door. And that's where she heard her daughter's unmistakable laughter in the wind. She looked around and decided to go investigate. Trenika closed the front door and descended the porch steps. She then walked around alongside the old brick house where Aryanna' s giggling met her ears every following step.

It was a nice sunny day outside. It was warm and comforting. But after what happened the day before, Trenika wondered if it was even safe to be out. That notion changed when Trenika made the journey around the back of the house and captured what lay before her eyes. Instantly, a smile appeared on her face as she watched her daughter run about in play of two beautiful Rottweiler puppies. For a moment, she just stood there leaning against the corner of the house gazing out at her precious child.

"It's beautiful, isn't it?" Came the reply of Jake who was sitting alone on the back porch.

"Jake," said Trenika with a start as she stepped around to climb the porch steps and join him.

She took a seat on the padded bench next to him while he puffed on his special pipe watching Aryanna. The old man reminded her of the actor Morgan Freeman. They shared the same features, the same humbled spirit, and he had the most intelligent eyes she'd ever seen. She also wondered what his story was.

"I didn't know you had dogs, Jake."

"I didn't," he said. "That boy of mines brought them home before dawn this morning. He said they were for baby girl and you."

"Oh. He's a real slick one," Trenika blushed.

"That he is." Jake chuckled. "But I love him like he's my own son, you know?"

"That's the story I wanna hear. How did you and Kaedon became committed?" She asked.

"One of the best days of my life after meeting my dear wife, Sylvia." Smiled Jake as he reencountered the day he met Kaedon for the first time.

As she listened, Trenika stared out at her loving daughter, thinking how blessed they were to have someone like Kaedon in their lives after all they've been through. Jake seemed to find enjoyment in his storytelling, believing God had placed Kaedon in his life to help him cope after losing his wife. The old man had just loss his wife of forty-one years two weeks before he had his heart attack. He had been left with a broken heart and wanted to go be with her again.

"But Kae stopped it from happening?"

"I guess the Lord saw fit that I shouldn't give up and to keep on living. That boy of mines had been there for me every step of the way."

"You didn't have children of your own?" She asked.

He shook his head. "Sylvia couldn't have children. We tried for years, but it just wouldn't happen. That almost tore us apart. To have my own family was everything I had hoped for."

"How did you two manage for so long?"

"Love and sacrifice," he answered.

Those two words hit home in her heart. She wanted more children herself, a whole house full of them, but not at the cost of them being affected and their father risking his health as well. Trenika had grown to complete her life with just Aryanna and their dreams. With Kaedon in their lives now, she wasn't sure how things would turn out for them.

"The sacrifice is the hardest part, Trenika. Loving someone is one thing, it's the nature of two hearts. But there comes a time where a sacrifice had to be made in order to love happily too."

"What was your sacrifice, Jake?"

Jake reached over and took her hand. He squeezed it and said, "My sacrifice was to stop dreaming of my own family and dream only of just being happy with my dear, Sylvia."

She understood him loud and clear. She'd made her sacrifice already, now it was up to Kaedon to see what his would be.

Or hasn't he done it already?

Chapter 12

Her name was Veronica Dunn. She was a high power trial lawyer whom Kaedon had known for quite some time now. She once represented him on a home invasion homicide case and won it fair and square. That was almost five years ago and since then her and Kaedon had become quite close. Kaedon didn't do white women but if he did, Veronica sure enough would have gotten her back blown out.

But at that moment, he needed Veronica like the air he breathed. She had clout in the judicial system department. Her father was the late Honorable Phillip Dunn, a circuit judge whose reputation never blemished. It was her who would save him right now from the double-murder rap he was wanted for. He needed a huge favor right here and he believed Veronica could make it happen.

"You're lucky I love your dimples, Kaedon, or else I wouldn't be risking my white ass to save yours."

"Just my dimples?" He smirked.

"Don't push it, buddy. However," Veronica shook her head in agitation as she sat behind the wheel of her BMW.

They were parked in a secluded spot way out in the St. Hebron area of the countryside away from the city slickers and the threat it posed in detaining him.

"I can do it, but you'll still have to do county time for the escape."

"I have no problem with that," he said.

"They gotta get something out of you for taking them through the hell you've created," said Veronica.

"How much county time?"

"Don't fret. I'll get right on it soon as I get back in town. The DA owes me one anyway. Just stay out of trouble until you hear from me."

"Okay," he was worried about Trenika and baby girl if he goes in for some county time. But he can count on Veronica to make sure they didn't bury him too.

"And about that name you gave me?" She added.

Romell. Kaedon frowned at the thought of the man who was now and enemy of his. Since the attempt on his life yesterday, Kaedon wondered if it was him that took a shot at him.

"What about him?"

"He's currently serving a three-year sentence for arson and felony battery. He already has seventeen months in."

"Are you sure we're talking about the same guy?" For some reason, Kaedon just couldn't believe that.

"Now you're questioning my integrity," she frowned.

Gripping the leather steering wheel with both hands, Veronica let out a breath and said, "I have a million other things of importance I could be doing than wasting my time with you, an idiot who doesn't even appreciate the loyalty I have for him."

"I appreciate you," he corrected.

"Get out!" She snapped. "I can't stand the looks of you right now."

"Close your damn eyes then," he kidded.

Veronica turned and punched him in the arm playfully, then reassured him that her research was accurate. Then, kicked him out of her car and left Kaedon in the dust. With a relieving sigh, Kaedon hurried back around the other side of the night club where Twan awaited him.

"What's the move, my nigga?"

Kaedon reached into the arm console between them where a Ziploc bag containing pre-rolled blunts of Kush were. He selected one of them and fired it up, filling his lungs with the weed smoke.

"Everything's gonna be alright, bro."

"But?" Twan looked at him.

Kaedon exhaled smoke in the air. "I may have to go do some county time for the escape shit."

"How much though?'

"I don't know how much yet."

"It's better than going to prison or death row for a fucking homicide," said Twan.

Kaedon nodded. "Way better."

"You got family to look after now, my nigga. That's what you need to be focused on," Twan spoke this from the heart, wanting the best for his main man.

And he was right, it's time to focus on family. Which is why he told Twan to take him to his girl.

"You could only be patient for so long," thought Ciera Crawford as she peered into the rearview mirror of her Ford Explorer.

She hadn't seen her brother in weeks and her patience had run thin. But first, she had to make sure she wasn't being followed as well. Because Kaedon was being blasted on all the surrounding news channels and radio stations. He was considered armed and dangerous, and every cop in the area was looking for him.

Although she knew the place where no one else would look for him at, probably except Twan and God himself, Ciera very much doubt he would be there. It was the last place that Kaedon would want to be found for fear of causing old man Jake to get in trouble too. She had to take her chances and see for herself. She only had an hour break from her job over at the County School Board Office, so she wasn't going to try any other place after that.

When she was sure that anyone wasn't following her, Ciera punched on the gas until she reached the area of her destination. Once she reached Jake's house and pulled her truck up to his fence in driveway, Ciera only saw his old Chevy truck parked out front. She got out and made her way to the front door and knocked on it. When the door was answered by another woman, it made Ciera suspicious as to who she were.

"Is Jake home?" She asked.

"You must be Ciera," Trenika said with a smile. "Yes, yes he's home. Come in." she stepped aside.

"Um, do I know you?" Ciera stepped over the threshold in her crème color skirt and blouse and flats, giving off the schoolteacher look to perfection.

"No. You don't. But I know a little about you."

"How so?'

"Your brother, Kaedon."

At the mention of her brother, Ciera sized the other woman up. Before she could reply she was rushed by two miniature monsters assaulting her feet with licks and sniffs. Then, came a pretty little girl that looked up at her with the most amazing brown eyes. Ciera had never known Jake's house to be so lively and busy as it was now other than when her and Kaedon and Twan was over. Suddenly, the old man appeared, and Ciera's heart gave a little flutter at the sight of him.

"Jake," Ciera stepped over the puppies bypassing Trenika and the child for the old man. "I just came to check on you and to see it you were okay."

"Yeah, right. Your brotha'll be here shortly." Jake gave her a reassuring look.

But when Ciera shot the other woman a hard look, Jake assured her that Trenika was aware of the situation. Then, he made introductions between both women and there was no pressure.

At ease now, Ciera took a seat on the sofa and one of the puppies approached her for some affection.

"I just finished making some sweet tea. I'll go bring you a glass." Trenika offered.

"You don't have to do that, Trenika."

"But I insist." Trenika left the room.

She looked almost happy to be in the company of Kaedon's sister.

"She's pretty," said Ciera.

"Your brotha has good taste." Smirked Jake.

"My brotha...? What are you saying, Jake?" Ciera needed some clarification on that statement.

"How about I let Trenika tell you herself. But allow me to warn you," said Jake. "They are a family now."

Those last five words were so profound that Ciera found it very hard to believe. Had her brother been hiding this woman and child from her all this time? Was the little girl her brother's daughter?

Trenika returned and handed Ciera her glass of sweet tea, then one to Jake, and then she took her place on the sofa across from the other woman with her glass in her hand.

"Are you ready for the truth, Ciera?"

Ciera nodded at her. "So, help me God," she said.

The old man shifted in his seat and got comfortable for this. Hell, this was better than his stories on TV. He had the best of the best right before him.

"Okay, Ciera?" Trenika replied.

"Yes," she was all ears.

Trenika looked her dead in her eyes. "Do you believe in love on first sight?" She asked.

And from there Ciera got the shock of her life as Trenika shared with her a story of love and war that had everything to do with the man they both loved.

A real love story.

The heart of a true gangsta.

Chapter 13

There was no emotion in Kaedon's eyes as he placed the pistol against the other man's head and pulled the trigger. Nor was there any when blood splattered on his face in the process. To kill a person, one must be empty of feelings because that could get you killed. Kaedon had to learn that the hard way at the beginning. Now, he was accustomed to it doing it, especially after being marked for death himself on some occasions.

Next, Twan pumped three slugs of his own into the chest of the already dead man. It was his way of showing Kaedon that they were in this together. The man of the hour was Andre Fuller, whom was the shooter from the day before. When Twan got word that Andre had been mysteriously shot in the arm and no one knew when or where the incident occurred, he put two and two together. And besides, Twan had been positive he had hit the shooter before ducked back into the getaway car. After lying in wait on Andre to exit the liquor store with the bottle of Seagram's Gin to ease his pain, they caught him slipping at the stop light on MLK Blvd just a while ago. They snatched him out of his car and tossed him into the trunk of another car and took to his final resting place.

Come to find out Vega had hired the hit, which was what Kaedon already figured. Now they had a lead or where to find Lonzo's other trusted goon, Poony, who was also Andre's getaway driver. Both were two of the same that

Kaedon and Twan saw with Lonzo the day before up on The Block. Once Poony gets his last wish denied then it was on to Vega. Saving the best for last always made vengeance taste so much better.

"We have to act fast because this one," said Twan.

It was legend that Poony had a reputation for putting in work all by his lonesome. Once a hitman for a former kingpin by the name of Grady, one who had ties with the Jamaican Shottaz Gang, Poony linked up with his big cousin Lonzo and redeemed his hustle. By now, Poony was probably searching for them to avenge Lonzo's death. But thanks to Andre, they had a lead that would put an end to Poony.

Kaedon said, "I need to get back to Trenika. We can catch this nigga later, bro."

"There might not be no later, Kae. If we don't put this dog down now, then we are taking the risk of him catching us slippin'"

"No."

"Just this one last shot, bro."

After they cleared the path from which they had taken to kill Andre in the woods, Kaedon headed straight for the car without a word. It wasn't that he was afraid of anything. He just wanted to make sure his family was straight. You could never be too careful in this game. Especially when dealing with a nigga like Poony, he was good at tracking niggas down where they least expect it. You can't sleep on a killer of his caliber.

Without another word on the matter, Twan took Kaedon back to the house. There at the house they both spotted Ciera's car in the driveway. Twan wanted to see her but thought better of it. He waited until his main man entered the house before he drove away. Twan wanted some action and since Kaedon didn't want to take that ride, he would do it himself. Shoot it wouldn't be the first time he had to go on a solo mission without his nigga.

The instant Kaedon entered the house, Aryanna shrieked with joy and ran over to him. He snatched her up and kissed her cheek. Then, he put her down and hurried down the hall to the bathroom. Kaedon spent about ten minutes in the shower washing away evidence of Andre's murder. Afterwards, he retreated to his room to put on clean clothes. By the time he was in clean underwear, Ciera was barging in the room with a curious expression on her face.

"What?" He looked up at her and said.

Ciera sat on the foot of the bed and shook her head in silent dismay.

"What?" Kaedon repeated.

"Are you really ready for that responsibility, Kaedon? Please let me know," she said.

A long silence passed before Kaedon decided to answer her question. This was someone who knew him better than anybody. So, Kaedon knew he had to choose his words wisely when talking to his sister.

"CeeCee, I've never been so sure of anything in my life than I am about Trenika and Ary," he said.

"So, this is final?"

"It's a chance for me to be happy."

"But you know once you make a commitment like this, you'll have to leave the streets alone? This will be your chance to start over and make things right. That little girl out there needs a real man to hold her down. All that street shit goes out the window."

"I get it," he said. "I understand."

Another brief silence in the air. Ciera had faith in her brother, she knew he had it in him to change. Maybe this is what he needed; it would be the answer to her prayers.

"To start over," Kaedon begins as he pulled on a pair of gray and black Nike ankle socks. "It would have to be somewhere different from here. I always wondered what it would be like to leave Quincy," he said.

"Where to, though?"

He shrugged. "Wherever she chooses to go."

"And about income? You leave the streets alone means having a real job now. No drug sellin'."

"I got a lil bit saved up," he said humbly.

"What's a little bit, Kaedon?"

"Damn CeeCee. Get the hell outta my pockets, girl. I got this under control," he said.

She nodded her understanding but still asked him what did he mean by he got a little bit saved up.

"I do too, but I just wanna know where I can help if I can."

"I don't need your money!"

"Hmph."

"I got a little over three hundred thousand dollars saved up, CeeCee."

"What!" His sister gasped.

"Hmph," he shrugged.

Ciera held out her hand and Kaedon gave her a low five slap.

"I don't want that shit, boy. I want money!"

"I got you. You know I'ma make sure you and my two nephews are straight. I haven't let y'all down yet and I don't plan to," he told her.

"We all we got," Ciera replied.

"We all we got."

Quietly standing outside the door listening in, Trenika wiped tears from her eyes. She placed her hand on her heart and sighed with content.

Back in the room, Kaedon finished getting dressed while his big sister eyed him with admiration. She had a newfound respect for her sibling. She wished there were more men like him in the world. One who wasn't afraid of change and walking a straight path.

"It's not gonna be easy though, sis," Kaedon replied as if reading her current thoughts.

She nodded. "Life never is, little brotha," she said. "Look at where we come from. We've had it hard all our lives, but we still made a way."

The bedroom door burst open, and Aryanna came running in laughing with one of her puppies on her heels. She ran and jumped right onto Kaedon's lap while squealing with pure glee. Kaedon was a natural with children and it warmed his big sister's heart to see him so happy now. Her brother was at peace. He was lucky.

"This who stole my heart first." Kaedon grinned and he tickled the child's ribs.

Aryanna was a giggling fit.

"And I can see why," said Ciera.

Then, she hugged and kissed her little brother before heading back off to work. Her conscience was clear; Kaedon was safe, and all was well. After seeing Ciera out, Trenika entered the room carrying the other puppy. She sat down on the bed where her daughter and Kaedon were still at play. Trenika then took her man by the hand.

"What's up?" He looked over at her.

"Nothing," she said as she cradled the puppy in the crook of her arm.

"Nothing, huh?" He gave her a mischievous grin.

"Nope." She tooted up her lips.

Kaedon eased over towards her. She reeled back from him cautiously, and then he pounced on her tickling her into a giggling fit too. When Aryanna joined, it was a riot of screams and laughter. It felt damn good to be happy for a change.

Kaedon can get used to this.

Until tragedy strikes again…

Chapter 14

Morning came in a flash, and when it did, it came with the news of two deaths. One in particular that rocked Kaedon's world in the worst way. The news of Twan getting killed the evening before at a local gas station. It was said that Twan had spotted Poony at a nearby Kelly Jr's gas station and confronted him. A gun battle transpired, and both men were shot several times and died at the scene. It was news that crushed Kaedon to the core. To hear of his main man getting killed was enough to drag Kaedon into a deep depression.

Kaedon was grief stricken, he wouldn't eat or sleep, all he did was cry for his dead homie. For days straight, Kaedon never left his room. Not even for Aryanna or his two nephews when Ciera brought them over to lift his spirits. But Trenika was there for her man, giving her all to soothe him, and he still wouldn't budge at all. The history that he and Twan shared together was like that of two blood related siblings. It had always been them who carried the weight on their shoulders together when the world got too cold. When they both loss their mothers, it was only each other they counted on to be strong. Then when Twan got jammed for that robbery at sixteen, it was Kaedon that offed the witnesses. Since that day, it was Twan and Kaedon. You see one, the other wasn't too far around. They were two peas in a pod, like Beavis and ButtHead. They were the package deal.

It was the fifth day. Kaedon finally came to his senses and got in the shower. He spent at least two hours in the bathroom crying what tears he had left in the shower. And when he emerged, Trenika was right there to do whatever he desired of her. And so she did, and faithfully, willingly opened herself up to him and let him pound his frustration and anger out until he had released all his energies upon her.

"I love you," she winced painfully as she laid there holding her man.

Trenika's pussy was swollen from his thug love. While Kaedon slept fitfully, she cooked him a nice meal and woke him up with dinner in bed.

"Who told you about this?" Kaedon said as he stared down at the plate filled with chicken pilau, yellow rice, cream corn, and a slice of pecan pie.

It was his favorite meal and there was no way he could say no to that.

"You told me Kae," she teased.

"I never told you about this," said Kaedon.

"Okay, okay, okay. I read it in that book you wrote. I found it beneath the bed while I was cleaning the room. I thought since you wrote about it then it must be a favorite dish of yours."

"My Grandma Lillie used to cook it for me," he said as he took a bite of the chicken.

Trenika watched him eat with pleasure, seeing that he enjoyed her style of cooking.

"Why didn't you tell me you were a writer?" She asked.

"It never crossed my mind."

"Well, I must say you are damn good at it. I actually enjoyed both books. I can tell most of your storylines came from personal experiences," said Trenika.

Kaedon said, "They were."

"And Sherry Lightfoot?" She was mentioning the name of a star character in one of his stories.

"My momma's character."

"Her story was deep. You ever thought about getting them published, baby?"

"Maybe one day," he said. "Where is Ary?"

"CeeCee took her to spend some time with the boys. I must say she misses you dearly. We all have. And I just want to say I'm sorry." Trenika laid her head upon his shoulder as he ate his food.

The food on his plate was demolished. Trenika was surprised and asked him if he wanted more. Kaedon nodded he did, and she was happy to go fix him another. Meanwhile, Kaedon rose up to his feet to stare at the reflection of himself in the mirror. It was time to make that concrete decision.

"You make sure you take a real good look at the man in from of you," came Jake's voice as he stood in the doorway.

He took a long, good look at the man in the mirror. What he saw was a man not content with the way his life was. Kaedon didn't want that street life anymore. The killing, drug selling, the whole aspect of being a gangsta. He didn't want that life for his new family. But that gangsta mentality would always be in him. It won't just go away completely, however, he could only pray that it didn't get in the way of his growing happiness. Old man Jake was a positive example of what a real man should be like. He wanted to make the old man very proud of him.

"You could never disappoint me, son. I knew what you was before you even realized what you was. I trust you to be nobody but Kaedon. All I'm asking you to do is look at the blessing of life you still have after all you've been through. That's all I'm saying son," Jake said to him before continuing on down the hall to the bathroom.

Trenika returned with another healthy plate of food and sat down on the bed beside him.

"Thank you," he said.

"Anything for my man," she smiled her winning smile and placed a kiss upon his cheek.

Today was one of the best days of her life since coming to Florida. To see her man back in his groove was a deep, heartfelt prayer answered. His downward spirit had been very hard on her lately.

"Pick any place in the world you want to go and start over and that's where we'll go. Any place," said Kaedon, surprising her with that unexpected statement.

Trenika looked at him long and hard before she even fixed her mouth to respond.

"Any place?"

"Wherever your heart desires," he added.

She shrugged.

"I've always wanted to go to New York and live," said Trenika in a slow drawl like she was unsure.

"Then, New York it is," he said.

"Really?" Her eyes lit up with astonishment.

He assured her that it was time for a change and what better way to do that than to start somewhere fresh? Although, he hated the cold weather, and New York had a history of blistering cold fronts; he was willing to man up, and deal with it if he meant making her happy. To Trenika, it felt too good to be true. Life taught her to never believe anything a man says until he proves himself worthy of the cause. She loved Kaedon, there was no question about that, but she wasn't fully healthy just yet to just place all her hopes and dreams into one bottle. Romell had really destroyed her peace of mind. She still had a lot of work to be done, and Lord knows she trusted Kaedon to fill those empty voids that have become her miserable life.

Two days before Twan's funeral, the authorities caught Vega trying to leave town on the expressway to escape the murder rap he was facing. Veronica had done as she had promised and now Kaedon was no longer a murder suspect. But he did have to go sit down for a while in jail, which is something he already anticipated.

To attend Twan's funeral was what he wanted most, and the judge granted him the furlough to do so. Afterwards, he had a long six months to a year of county time he had to do. But Kaedon wasn't sweating the small time; his only concern was leaving Trenika and Aryanna behind. His family was what was most important to him. So, after the ceremony at the burial gravesite, after throwing dirt, and a red rose onto Twan's casket, Kaedon turned around and extended his arms to be cuffed. No sense in wasting time, his mind was made up already.

It took some very strong will power to watch them take her man away without acting a fool. But Trenika was already prepared for what she hated to see happen. The only thing she did was blow him a kiss and mouthed the words "I love you" as Kaedon was being escorted away to jail. There was plenty of tears that day, even a few shed by old man Jake. It was the last thing that he wanted to see go down, but Kaedon's doing what he had to do was for the best. For the best of his life would be like once he becomes a free man again.

For the next several months, Kaedon planned to utilize his time in the county jail to pen himself another story, better himself as a man, and prepare for a beautiful future that was ahead of him. In the process, Trenika would be there every step of the way. She would not miss one visit, never go one day without writing him, and make sure his canteen was straight. She was ready to ride with her man and prove to him that she could stand firm. The only hard part about it all was Aryanna, who had grown so attached to Kaedon that her behavioral patterns had become worser by the day of him being gone. And it was a blow to his pride that he had to leave her again. But after the visits became regular and Aryanna was able to see him at least twice a week, the child grew to understand that this much is what she could get for now. Aryanna had become that link that kept their connection together and the motivation for Kaedon to get the fuck out of there.

Even before, jail time wasn't nothing to Kaedon because he knew he was getting out to the same ole street game. He had something different now to look forward to, a reason to remain adequate in order to get back free to his family. By the fifth month down, Trenika had changed her mind about New York saying that she remembered Romell telling her about him having relatives that lived there. The possibility of him bumping into her there was all the reason why she no longer desired the Big Apple. But little did she know that Kaedon had plans for Romell when he got out of prison. He vowed that after taking care the man who had caused Trenika so much pain and agony, he would be completely done with killing. Not unless he had no other choice but to kill to protect his family. Romell won't even have a clue that he would be stalked from the moment he stepped out those prison gates until he was lying zipped up in a bodybag. As long as he was alive, Trenika would never be comfortable. He had to die in order for Kaedon to have his woman completely.

"So, what is your second choice?" Kaedon asked.

"Atlanta," Trenika answered.

They were staring at one another through the thick plexiglass in the visiting area.

"I also remember you saying you're originally born in Georgia."

"Cairo, Georgia. The Hotbed," he said.

"Syrup makers, right?"

He nodded. "That's what Grandma Lillie said."

Then, it was Georgia that they planned to go and raise their family. It was good that way because then they would still be close to Ciera and the boys and Jake.

"I can't wait," Trenika said.

"Me too."

Kaedon was sure that they would have a nice life in Georgia.

By the end of his stay there in the county, Kaedon would have done seven months total. He had missed his family so much that it was driving him insane. It was up until that moment Kaedon realized just how much having a family and devoting his life and honor to them was worth. He was more than ready to set that positive example that was believed of him to do. Life was too short to be bullshitting around where there was so much of it to enjoy. Kaedon wanted to live. He just wanted to finally be happy.

Chapter 15

A year later, Kaedon sat comfortably behind the wheel of his Lincoln Aviator waiting on the last bell to ring so he could retrieve his daughter. Aryanna was five now, so bright and beautiful. His pride and joy. He had taken him a whole lot of patience and love to raise such a child.

Two minutes before the bell rang, Kaedon exited the truck and waited out in the open. This was his normal routine since his baby girl started attending school. From Pre-K to the first grade, Kaedon was always on time retrieving Aryanna. When the final bell rang, there was a brief moment of silence, then there was an explosion of children actively readying themselves to go home. School kids poured from every outlet there was, heading for their school buses and waiting parents and relatives to come scoop them up.

In the midst of waiting for baby girl to show up, Kaedon's attention was stolen by the presence of a silver Genesis GV80 pulling upon the scene. This was his first time ever seeing the car, at which he wondered who it was actually driving such a car as that. Whoever it was, had to be getting to the money bag to afford a ride like that one.

"Umm, excuse me, sir?" A voice replied behind him.

Kaedon turned at the familiar voice and smiled at the sight of Aryanna and her preciousness.

"You mind tellin' me where I can find my personal driver to take me home?" Said Aryanna.

Widening his smile, Kaedon reached for his baby girl's backpack and said, "I'm at your service."

"Well thank you, sir," she said politely playing her role.

"You're welcome, miss." Kaedon walked her around to the passenger side and lifted her up to settle in the big truck.

As he made his way back around to the other side, Kaedon looked in the direction of the Genesis and spotted a female now standing next to it. She didn't look familiar to him, but she definitely was rocking the latest fashion. Once inside the truck and making sure baby girl had her seatbelt on, Kaedon started the engine and rolled out. In passing, he met the female's gaze and for an instant he would have sworn he saw her wink at him.

Since arriving in Atlanta a little over a year ago, there has never been an occasion where another female caused him to betray his trust with Trenika. Though there have been many who tried to make him stray, his loyalty was immovable. However, he appreciated a beautiful woman who was on top of her shit. But never in a way where his love for Trenika is to be questioned for any reason. Besides his own woman was very much on top of her game. Trenika was making a good name for herself as an artist that some of her pieces had reached some big-time art galleries way up in New York. From the Whitney Museum of American Art of New York to Palm Beach International Contemporary Art & Design Gallery, she was doing her thing. A few of her paintings helped purchase the stucco-styled four bedroom home that they now had out in East Cobb, Atlanta. They went from living in an apartment on Maryland Drive to living it up in a house of their own five months later. Plus, Trenika was an active caregiver for the elderly when she wasn't painting. So, to step out on such a catch as her, Kaedon would be a damn fool. Their life was beautiful together, and Kaedon wouldn't have asked for a better situation.

"Ms. Rowe is stupid," Aryanna said,

"What I told you about calling people out of their names, Ary?" Said Kaedon sternly.

"But she is, Kae," She argued.

"Okay, baby girl." He drew a deep breath. "What did she do to make you feel that way?"

Kaedon knew that the person named Ms. Rowe was baby girl's art teacher, and they been beefin' ever since Aryanna clowned her in front of the class about her not knowing how to paint. The issue today was Ms. Rowe being prejudiced towards Aryanna by saying that she couldn't participate in the art contest next Friday because her skills in art were too advance than the rest of the class. That she didn't want the other school kids complaining about going up against someone whose mother is a professional artist. The real meaning of the matter is that Aryanna had a thing about bragging about her mother's artwork that her very own art teacher has become irritably annoyed about the whole situation. Ms. Rowe was being a hater on every level.

"I'll see about that myself." Frowned Kaedon as he told baby girl he was going to back to give the art teacher apiece of his mind.

He hit the blinkers in preparation to make a U-turn back towards the school. Like the little lady that she has become, Aryanna reached over and patted his arm smoothly.

"Don't worry about her, Kae. Don't get in no trouble. She is still stupid," she said.

If it wasn't for those words, Kaedon would have gone back to the school and raised pure hell.

Fifteen minutes later, they pulled into the driveway of their gated residence. Kaedon parked the truck before the two-car garage, which was empty except for the '69 Chevy Camaro that he was working on inside. He had a thing for older model cars and this one exactly had belong to Twan before he died. Twan was in the process of building the car from scratch and to honor his main man's work, Kaedon decided to do it on his own. The car was a monster, and Kaedon couldn't wait until the whole thing was completed.

Aryanna opened the door and jumped down before Kaedon could come around and assist her. She was home now, and this was her kingdom. Together they made themselves over to the front door of the house. Upon opening the front door, both Eightball and LuLu bound outside into the bright lit sunshine almost knocking Kaedon and Aryanna over in the process. The two Rottweiler puppies were now two massively built machines and just as vicious as they come. Eightball, who has a brown circular patch of fur over his right eye, had the head the size of a full grown bull's. The dog was so big he looked like a miniature tank. And LuLu wasn't no slight neither, which was Aryanna best friend and could get dangerously volatile when it comes to baby girl. Sometimes she and Kaedon be battling for Aryanna's attention. LuLu was the real queen of the house and even Trenika would not tell you differently.

While both dogs ran about the front lawn to do their business, Kaedon stood there on the doorstep observing them. The dogs were well-trained and very disciplined. It was then the front door of the house opened next door, and a stocky built Cuban-looking guy stepped out to smoke a cigarette. Every time Kaedon looked at the guy, he always thought the man was too quiet and curious for his comfort. But the issue didn't just stop with him; it was the rest of the blended family that lived in that same house. The other were middle aged white male, a pretty respectful looking older black woman, and two children: a boy and a girl. Since they moved in about two months ago, Kaedon can't even count on both hands how many times he actually saw the rest of the family leave the house other than spend some time out back behind the house near the pool. There was something strange about their whole existence.

When the Cuban glanced in Kaedon's direction, he shrugged and turned away from him. He called for the dogs, and they came galloping towards the front door. LuLu went straight through while Eightball halted on the doorstep and turned completely around as if to stand guard over the entrance of his domain.

"Let's go boy!" Kaedon rubbed Eightball's large head and stepped through the door inside the house. Eightball entered next and the door was closed shut behind him.

Meanwhile, Trenika was making her last rounds checking on her patients before heading home to cook dinner for her lovely family. Her last stop before home was to see one of her favorites over in Glenwood Road. His name was Vincent 'Vince' Montgomery, also a war veteran, and a retired mixed Martial Arts instructor who had some amazing stories to tell. As she pulled up outside Vince's home in her Infiniti G35 and seeing three other vehicles parked outside, Trenika only recognized one of the cars as belonging to Renee, who was Vince's beloved granddaughter. After parking her car and getting out to go do her deed, Trenika was enroute towards the front door when her cellphone rang. It was Lisa calling, and no matter how bad she wanted to send her girl straight to voicemail, she didn't. She retrieved the phone from the pocket of her jeans and killed the "Hoochee Mama" ringtone by answering the phone.

"It's official," came Lisa's voice.

"What's official, girl?"

"Really? Like we wasn't just talkin' about the shit two nights ago! Byron, bitch!"

"What about him?" Trenika rolled her eyes as she ascended the steps onto the front porch of the house.

"He just proposed to me! I can't believe it! Baby. I got a big ass rock on my finger right now!" Lisa squealed joyously through the phone that Trenika had to pull it away for a moment before she damaged an eardrum.

"Ohmigod!" Trenika beamed brightly, happy for her girl.

After nearly three and a half years with Bryon Reynolds, it was about time he popped the question. Just hearing this made her think of Kaedon and the love they shared together. Now she wondered when will he be up for popping that magical question next. It really didn't matter to her because she was happy just as long as they were together.

"I'm sending you a pic of the ring now, girl! You have to come back home to celebrate with me, sis. Please?"

"I will soon, sis, just not right now," she told her.

"Don't make me wait forever and a day, Nika!"

"I won't." Trenika promised. "I won't."

She had to cut the phone call short because she needed to get inside to check on Vince. They promised to chat later on tonight when all has settled. After hanging up with her girl, reached up to knock on the door, but the door opened the instant she made contact with it, revealing a tall, dark and handsome creature of a man. Trenika swallowed down the lump in her throat and quickly regained her sense of self-conduct.

"I'm here to see Mr. Vince. I'm his caregiver," Trenika replied in a light tone.

"And you are…?" The man wanted to know.

"Trenika," she extended her hand in greeting.

The man looked at her hand like it wasn't clean and turned his gaze back up to meet hers.

"I'm sorry, but I don't think that would be necessary now, giving that Uncle Vince has passed away this afternoon.

"Excuse me? He did what?" Trenika heart quickened.

"Died," he said simply.

For a brief moment, Trenika's head dropped in sorrow, then she looked up at the man through tearful eyes. Then without warning shoved him aside and let herself through the door of the house calling for the old man. The house seemed to be empty of Vince's presence, and any other presence as well, other than the tall, dark, and handsome presence still standing at the front door. The man watched silently as Trenika hurried from one room to the other in search of Vince. A minute later when she came trudging back up to the front of the house, all her energy seemed to have drained out of her.

Trenika went over to Vince's favorite rocking chair and sat down in it. Then, she buried her face inside her hands and cried.

"Oh Vince," she sobbed softly.

Still shadowing the doorway with his large presence, the man shook his head sadly and left her sitting there crying her eyes out. When the door shut behind him, Trenika lifted her head and just let her tears run free. She just rocked and cried and rocked and cried. The old man reminded her so much of Jake.

Chapter 16

Kaedon was pissed with her for breaking her promise. Trenika promised him that she wouldn't grow a personal attachment with her patients, and she did. He knew eventually it was gonna come down to this. Kaedon just didn't know that it would be this soon.

For the next couple of days, Kaedon watched his woman come and go with that saddened look in her eyes. He knew she cared about the old man a great deal, and that he reminded her of Jake at times, which he totally understood; but still didn't like the fact that she grew attached. When her period of grief had passed, Trenika was back to her old self again. But once again, she and Kaedon had to have a serious talk about emotions. That Friday night, Kaedon decided to take his girls out to the movies to watch something called Puss In Boots that Aryanna was very adamant about seeing. Kaedon was all for it, especially if it would make Trenika feel much better after her recent loss of a dear friend. So, they all got dressed in their finest wear and headed out to the AMC Theaters at the local mall. This was one of the pleasures of having a family where you could have your own night out after a busy week to go watch a movie and just enjoy the vibes.

"I know what you're up to," Trenika said to Kaedon with that mischievous smirk of hers.

"What?" He pretended to be clueless as Aryanna stood in front of him waiting in line for popcorn and treats and whatever else that she desired.

Before Trenika could respond, she was interrupted by the sudden presence of Mario and Mo'Nique, and both of their little girls. Mario was Kaedon's cousin from Cairo who now resided in Atlanta to teach music at the local high school. Mario was cool peoples and his family was beautiful, which is why Kaedon and Trenika were more acceptive towards them than anybody else.

"How it going, cuz?" Mario approached.

"You see it," Kaedon said humbly as he bumped fists with Mario in greeting.

And just like that Trenika was conversing with Mario's wife, Mo'Nique, who was an amazing real estate agent. And the sweet little girls, Aryanna, didn't waste no time commanding the attention of them and the others. But after catching the attention of others who were standing in line waiting and receiving a few stubborn looks at the assumption that Mario and his family was cutting in line, Trenika peeped the play and shooed the two men off. She said that she'll order them and the girls from her own pocket. From there, the two cousins stepped over inside the game arcade area which was busy with children. Kaedon quicky straddled one of the motorcycle games that was vacant. Mario got on the bike next to him and they both gave each other a challenging glance.

"Whatcha say? You wanna run one, cuz?"

Kaedon grinned. "You ain't saying nothin', cuz! This is what I do for real," he said.

"Well, let's see then, big mouth." Mario reached in his pocket for a quarter.

Kaedon did the same and punched a quarter into the slot to start the game. It was moments like these that Kaedon had forgotten all about. The streets had been so demanding that he never had the time to really be that kid he once was.

At an early age, Kaedon had taken on the role as being the black sheep of his family. It was very rare that he had fun like this growing up. Before his mother died when he was just ten years old, he had a great upbringing because she made sure he lived a normal childhood. But anything after that, all the fun and games had come to a cease. At eleven years old, Kaedon was already skipping school and running errands for the street hustlers in his hood. Grandma Lillie could only do so much to save him, but Kaedon didn't want saving. He wanted to do what he wanted and needed to do to escape the pain of losing his dear mother.

Now that evening, at that very moment, Kaedon realized how much fun it was to finally be clear of all the bullshit and focus on enjoying life. Simple things as riding an electronic arcade motorcycle was enough to make him appreciate simplicity.

"You don't want none, cuz!" Kaedon said excitedly, moments before winning first place.

He roared and threw his hands up in victory. Mario laughed and gave him a high five after coming in second place.

"When you get some free time on your hands come over to the house. That way we can ride on the real deal," suggested Mario.

"You got a bike?" Kaedon asked.

"Two of them to be exact. It's what I do for real, cuz!" Grabbing ahold of the handle bars again and leaning forward on the bike, Mario made the sound of a motorcycle zooming through traffic.

"Y'all two knuckleheads ready?" Said Mo'Nique from behind them with the rest of the girls.

Both Kaedon and his cousin dismounted the bikes and reached to relieve their women of the food and drinks. Stealing a kiss from his woman, Kaedon led the way out of the arcade.

During the middle of the movie, Kaedon excused himself to go to the restroom. Aryanna told him to hurry back, and he promised that he would. He stroked Trenika's chin and hurried to pee. A minute later, Kaedon burst through the door of the restroom and straight to the urinal. Trenika had told him earlier about drinking all those sodas in one day. But he couldn't help it. He was crazy over Mountain Dew soda, which is what Aryanna made sure he got a tall cup of for the movie that night. Afterward, he washed his hands quickly and made his way for the door. Before he reached the door it opened suddenly, and two young white kids came hurrying in. Seeing them made him remember back when he and Twan were just boys their age. They would skip school just to go to the movies, pay for a movie, and watched at least three movies back to back before leaving. They used to hide out in the restroom until the other movies started. Back then, Kaedon and his main man used to do all types of crazy stuff together. Exiting from the restroom, Kaedon headed back to where he left the girls.

"You're missing the good part, Kae!" Aryanna said the instant he reclaimed his seat next to her.

"How you know it's the good part?"

"Shh. Kaedon. Watch the movie!" Aryanna handed over her stale popcorn so he could eat and stop talking over the movie.

From the other side of baby girl, Trenika was holding in her laugh. Kaedon looked over and threw a handful of popcorn at her. For the rest of the movie, Kaedon kept his mouth shut and watched it with open enjoyment. When it was over, he could actually say that he liked the little alcoholic cat with the sword. While some stayed back to watch the credits, Kaedon took baby girl up in his arms and carried her out alongside his woman. Aryanna had been fighting sleep up until the very end. In the morning, he would tell her how the cat eventually saved the day against the villain.

Outside, in the wake of everybody slowly making their exit out of the mall, Kaedon looked to see if he could spot Mario and his family. They hadn't watched the same movie as them, but still he wanted to make sure that they made it out okay.

"Professor Newman! Mr. Newman?" Bellowed a tall, lanky black girl who appeared as though she was looking in Kaedon's direction and approaching as well.

Kaedon placed a hand on the back of baby girl's head as she rested her face in the crook of his neck asleep. As he continued to press on towards the door with the moving crowd, Kaedon happened to look up again at the proximity of the girl closing in on him.

"Professor Newman. It's me, Stephanie Maddox. From your history class," said the tall pretty girl.

"Um, I don't know what you're talking about. I think you got the wrong person," Kaedon replied and continued to push on forward outside.

"Really, sir?" Stephanie followed. "I mean, I'm sorry for interrupting your evening and all, but I need your input on something before the upcoming test exam. However, I was hoping you could approve my...Professor Newman?" The girl named Stephanie paused and gave Kaedon this open, weird look. "Why you look so different?"

"Because I'm not who you think I am," Kaedon snapped but not too much in a vicious way.

"Where do you go to school at, honey?" Trenika decided to cut in and pan things out.

She knew if the girl kept trying then it would eventually run Kaedon's patience thin and then he would really go the fuck off.

"I'm a sophomore at Georgia Tech majoring in English Literature and History. I'm only here in Atlanta visiting friends for the weekend. I thought after seeing Professor...I wanted some input on something I would like to do for my history exam project. But I guess I'll never know now, or unless you would like to run it across your twin brother for me?" Said Stephanie.

"Twin brotha?" Kaedon hissed darkly. "Little girl—"

"I'm sorry, Stephanie. There's been an honest mistake. You have a nice evening, sweet one." Trenika pushed Kaedon forward and told him to focus on what's ahead.

"Was that lady crazy, Daddy?" Came Aryanna groggy voice as she lifted her sleepy gaze up at him.

Kaedon stopped suddenly at the fact of baby girl calling him daddy. You know how long he'd been waiting to hear her say that word? But he couldn't enjoy the moment long before he answered, "Damn right she is!" And Trenika continued shoving him forward.

Trenika just wanted to get in the car, get home, and get in bed with her man.

"She called me daddy," Kaedon said excitedly the moment they were in traffic.

"Just let it flow with its own current baby. I know you're happy about it, but just let it flow." Trenika took his hand and squeezed it as he drove them home for the night.

"Baby girl called me daddy!" Kaedon said to himself.

Hearing her say that means they were progressing, although Aryanna probably won't remember ever saying it later. But that was all good because hearing it that one time was perfect enough for Kaedon. Things like that really make a gangsta proud.

Chapter 17

Two days later while taking a nap on the living room sofa, Trenika woke up instantly, bolting upright with a gasp as though she had just experienced a nightmare. But it wasn't a nightmare from a long shot, though it did seemed strange that she had had such a dream.

Eightball lifted his large head from the floor next to the sofa with those big golden curious eyes. LuLu was nowhere in sight but certainly was not that far. Throwing her bare pedicured feet over the side of the sofa next to Eightball's big, muscled butt, Trenika stood up and padded over into the spacious kitchen. She retrieved a drinking cup from the cupboard and ran herself a little tap water and staring out of the kitchen window, something caught her eye. It was the house next door, the only woman of the house, the suspicious one, she too was staring out of her kitchen window. The woman appeared to be staring in a daze.

Trenika lifted her hand and waved, her movement caught the woman's attention, she snapped out of her dazed, smiled, and waved back. Then just like that her smile disappeared and the woman vanished from the window.

"Weird as hell!" Trenika thought to herself regarding the woman whom she has yet to speak to.

Once before when the new family first arrived, Trenika thought it was best to go over to introduce herself. But the big stalky Cuban guy answered the door and explained that the woman of the house wasn't feeling well. It was the way he said it that made her believe it was a lie. He wasn't polite about it at all, nor did he seem sincere in his words. So, Trenika walked back over to her house and continued doing whatever she was doing. Since then, Trenika only seen flashes of the woman in passing, even with those of her family as well. The only explanation Trenika could think of was that the people next door were either hiding from something or they were some type of strange cult.

Speaking of strange, Trenika set her cup down on the kitchen counter and took her exit. From there she went into her art room which was two times bigger than the one in her old home. This one she had added a space for a little corner office to which she had sat before her desk and powered on her laptop computer. This is what her dream minutes ago led her to do. Trenika did not think it was possible that there was another, but every thought, occurrence, or action was a possibility that which could change one's perspective.

Professor Newman, Trenika typed as she engaged her search engine of Georgia Tech's administration staff or whatever she could find. LuLu appeared in the doorway of the art room and the heaviness of her footfalls and the jingling from her nametag of her collar caught Trenika's attention. Trenika turned and warned LuLu to not come in the room or she would kick her ass. She didn't want no animals in her art room and LuLu should already know that. LuLu ignored her warning and still entered the room to come perch down next to her swivel chair.

"Oh. My. Fucking. God!" Trenika drew in breath the instant shock as her hands flew up to her mouth in surprise at what laid before her eyes.

"No. No. No. No. No! This can't be true. Hell no!" She replied.

But it was true indeed. The man staring into the computer screen at her indeed was Professor Zaman Newman, but he also had the identical face of none other than Kaedon Smith. Enlarging the photo to make sure her eyes wasn't deceiving her, Trenika eyes widen with the unmistakable truth of what she was seeing at that very moment was a cold hard reality. Kaedon did have a twin brother, and the proof of that matter sat right there before her eyes.

She read: Professor Zamon Newman was a junior professor of History and Public Administration. The son of Rose and Hezachi Newman, both who served as a General Counsel in the state government of Albany, Georgia and as a state retirement commissioner. Professor Newman is also married to his high school sweetheart, Melody Simone Newman, professional director of the performing arts, and the devoted mother of their beloved newly arrived little son.

As Trenika continued to read, her eyes brimmed up with tears of agony, because she knew how much this was going to hurt Kaedon. It was going to break his heart into millions of pieces. Here it was after thirty years of living, Kaedon finds out that he has an identical twin brother. He was going to feel betrayed. Betrayed by everyone he thought he ever loved.

Suddenly, the front door opened and both Aryanna and Kaedon announced their presence. Trenika thought fast and powered off the computer and rose up to her feet to meet her family. Before making her exit, she wiped at her eyes, took a few deep breaths, and stepped out to go see what her two loves brought home.

For several days since learning about Kaedon's mysterious twin brother, Trenika had wrestled with the thought of telling him. She was not only afraid of him brushing her off about such nonsense but also seeing the pain in his eyes once he realized she wouldn't dare play with him like that. Because a situation like this could cause a man all types of conflicting emotions that could turn very dangerous.

Giving the gangsta mentality that Kaedon had been working on so hard on trying to put to bed completely, it would only awaken something much more vicious instead. So, before Trenika made the scary decision to tell her man the truth, she decided to go confront the truth which was the mysterious twin brother herself. And that's exactly what Trenika found herself doing on that Thursday afternoon by walking the premises of the Georgia Tech University for the very first time in her life. Having received and Associate in Arts degree back over in New Orleans at Xavier University, she knew what the college life feels like. She also received a Bachelor of Arts degree in Psychology as well, so Trenika wasn't dumb from a long shot. She just had a lot of bad experiences in her life that caused her heavy grief. Now, here she was at thirty-five years old walking about a college campus looking just as young and healthy as all the rest of the students present.

"Excuse me?" Trenika stopped some goofy-looking black kid who appeared as though he was smart enough to help her out. "I'm looking for Professor Newman's History class. Could you please help me?" She asked.

"You're in luck. I'm headed in that direction," said the black kid who also looked like he didn't have a lot of popular college friends with the way he was promoting the Steve Urkel look, but in new form.

The kid had the geekiness written all over him.

"Are you in his History class?" Trenika questioned.

"I'm associating in Mathematics and Computer science. I was already going that way to meet my girlfriend," the kid smirked up at her as he led the way.

"And what is her name?" Trenika figured he was lying just so that he could be seen walking around with a classy bitch. Not that she was conceited or anything, she was just stating the obvious of what's going on.

"Her name is Camilla McNeil."

"And yours?"

"Jeremy," he said proudly. "Jeremy Vance."

After about a few turns and a stretch of a walkway, the kid Jeremy was met by a young pretty brown skin girl with cute pink braces in her mouth. He then hugged her and introduced her as his girlfriend, Camilla, but grinning the whole time as though he had read her mind earlier. Trenika stood corrected and complimented Jeremy on his taste of a pretty girlfriend. Next, Trenika was directed to the next building over to her right where she was assured she would find who she was looking for. As she approached the building, Trenika willed herself to stay calm.

She entered the building and after a few wrong turns and damn near colliding with two other female students, Trenika let herself into the door of a class that was already in session. The room was very spacious with what looked like a hundred students in attendance. Upon her entrance, Professor Newman glanced up at her from where he stood down upon the platform presenting his lecture on Benjamin Franklin recommendation of the historical Bray School that taught both free and enslaved black children from 1760 to 1774. It was said to be the oldest surviving schoolhouse since the 18th century.

After finding her a seat way in the back if the class, Trenika removed her smartphone from her pants pocket and began recording. She wanted to not catch only her now visual shock but the actual truth on footage. Professor Newman was indeed every spit of the mirror image of Kaedon, from the low cut with the deep waves to the body structure of a man well-fit. The only difference was that the professor wore glasses, and Kaedon wouldn't get caught dead wearing any kind. Overall, the God honest truth was standing there before her eyes, and Trenika could only pray that this situation does not cause her to lose what she'd worked so hard for.

Chapter 18

The relationship between Kaedon and his cousin Ranaja aka Naja was special. Although he was a year older than her, it still didn't change the fact that they were so much alike. Naja, who was originally from Tallahassee, which was just only a few miles from where Kaedon grew up in Quincey, had relocated to Atlanta years ago to pursue this girl she like. They stayed together for a couple of years before Naja shot the bitch in the face for disrespecting her.

A gangsta bitch she was. Naja was fearless was they come and smarter than the average hustler. Despite her way of life, it was people like her that kept Kaedon on top of his game. From a gangsta to another, Naja carried hers better than some niggas hands down. But she wasn't your rip and running the streets type of bitch that sought attention. Naja had long shed that personality in exchanged for a businesswoman mindset. The owner of two beauty shops, a weed dispensary, and a daycare nursery; Naja seemed to have it all figured out which is why Kaedon was riding shotgun in her shiny money green CLS Mercedes Benz. It was time to talk about investment, and he wanted to see what options he had regarding what she had in mind.

During weekdays, he worked from six to two as a part-time sand and gravel contractor. It was an honest job but after doing that for a year, Kaedon wanted to progress in developing his own business.

"You know what I've been really wanting to do though, cuz?" Naja replied, pulling on her cigarillo blunt of Girl Scout Cookie weed and inhaling deeply.

"What's that?" Kaedon was blowing on his own bud as he sat decked out in Versace linen.

"Owning my rig," said Naja. "I'm hearing the truckin' business is a very lucrative business."

Now she was talking his language, thought Kaedon. Back down in Quincy, one of his partners owned a rig or two and was pulling profitable contracts with some big businesses. Even back then when he was in the game, he considered investing in the trucking business. Plus, he was even considering going to school to get his CDL license so that he could push his own truck.

"Do it," Naja encouraged him. "While you study to get your CDL, I'll be hunting for the nicest truck. My boy Mitch would know where to look," she said.

"Sounds like a plan to me."

"Are you sure you really wanna do this, cuz? Because being a truck driver you stand the risk of being on the road for days or a week at a time."

"I know what I'm up against, Naja."

"Then it's settled."

However, he still would consult Trenika about all this because he wanted them to be on the same page. They were cruising down I-285 exit to Buckhead Highway and turned into the entrance of a local BP station. Naja parked her Benz next to a gas pump just as a cocaine white Porshe Cayenne Bi-Turbo pulled up on the other side of the gas pump on Kaedon's side.

"That's that crazy bitch, Kelly," Naja pointed out.

"Who is she?" Kaedon recognized her from the school that day when he went to pick baby girl up.

Today, she had her short blond Halle Berry hairdo going on. Naja donned on her $1,000 Gucci sunglasses and looked straight ahead.

"She just came home from the Feds after doing five years. She was fuckin' with this big dopeboy outta Zone 6 that the Feds snatched up and burnt down his whole empire. Word on the streets is that Kelly kept it solid and didn't fold on them niggas."

"And her nigga?" He asked.

"Gone for a very long time. He won't ever see the other side again if the Feds got anything to do with it," Naja said before opening the door and getting out.

With her expensive Marc Jacobs clutch in hand, Naja strutted her shit like the dime piece she was. And so was Kelly, who too was evenly bad but with a little more thickness. All Kaedon could do was shake his head as he watched both women walk it out like the beautiful black queens they were. Naja in her Fendi Couture suit and Kelly in her Tory Burch sandals, they both had it going on. But its who would be more ladylike and open the door for the other is what Kaedon wanted to see. A moment later, Kelly reached for the door first and opened it for Naja to enter. When Naja went inside, Kelly shot a quick glance over her shoulder in his direction and winked. Then, she entered, knowing Kaedon was watching, and knowing it was only a matter of time. Right then Kaedon pulled out his phone and sent his woman an "I Love You" text with a funny card attached. It wasn't out of guilt for watching another woman, for he does things like that on the daily. Anything it takes to make her smile; he was all for it.

"So, you did come," said Professor Zamon Newman when the last of his students exited through the door. "I was expecting to see him instead of you."

"So, you know who I am?" Trenika asked as she remained sitting where she had been since entering the room. She had listened to him teach for the next thirty minutes up until just a few minutes ago. With the time she had to observe the man and make her comparisons, Trenika had to give it to him; he was quite a character. The man was ridiculously charming without effort.

"As of Monday morning, when I was approached after class by one of my students with this unnerving explanation of her bumping into a mysterious twin brother that I've had no clue ever existed," said the professor, having gathered up his papers and secured them into his leather briefcase before finally making his approach.

"You don't seem surprised," said Trenika.

"I'm quite surprised to be exact," he answered as he ascended the steps to where she sat.

He eased into a seat two chairs over from where Trenika's eyes seem to bore right through him for some reason.

"I didn't believe it at first, of course, but when young Stephanie showed me the few photos that she'd taken of you two, I became convinced that I've been living a lie this whole damn time."

"Felt betrayed by those you love."

"Exactly," he nodded.

Trenika got up and closed the distance between them and sat directly next to him. Now looking at the professor this up close and personal was freaky in a sense. It was as if her and Kaedon was role playing or something. However, he would never pretend he's someone he's not. Kaedon was a gangsta through and through, and no one in the world could tell him differently.

"So, how do you think my husband would feel when he does learn that he's been betrayed as well?"

"I don't know who your husband is," he said. "Nor do I know you for that matter."

"Well," she replied humbly. "Let me tell you a story."

Trenika never took her eyes away from her man's mysterious twin brother. Then, she told him about the day she met Kaedon and how loving him changed her life for the better. She wanted this man to know that not only was Kaedon a gangsta but a man of honor also. As he listened,

Trenika showed him pictures from her phone's photo gallery of the man she loved more than she ever thought she was capable of loving again. But it was the photos that Zamon saw of Aryanna and Kaedon together that made his heart warm.

"I know you have your own life to live but I just wanted you to know that there's another part of you out there that deserves to know you exist," Trenika replied with the most tenderest voice.

"Wanna know what crazy?" said Zamon.

"What?"

"That I somehow always knew there was another part of me out there somewhere," he said. "Like there was something missing, a feeling of something...I don't know how to explain it."

"A spiritual connection or something?"

"Something. Like I knew he was there, that brotherly connection, but I couldn't put a title on it until just now. I'm aware of the special connection that twins have, and I think that's what it was; but not really knowing why that feeling existed." Zamon slowly shook his head in silent weary.

"I understand," she whispered.

A momentary silence hung in the air between them and at that moment no words seemed to matter. What's understood don't need to be explained. It was time for Trenika to get back to the house and break the news to her man.

"So, when can I finally meet him?"

Trenika stood up.

"Soon."

He rose up to his feet next.

"Okay. I'm not gonna confront my parents until I've met my twin brother personally myself," he said.

"Sounds like a plan." Trenika borrowed one of her man's phases and extended her hand.

"You never told me your name." Zamon reminded her.

"Trenika," she said. "Trenika Smith."

Chapter 19

That very same evening when Trenika arrived home, she entered the house to Eightball bullying Aryanna around in the family room on the floor while she was trying to watch educational videos on her mini pro tablet. Stretched out on the sofa with a Truckin' n Buckin' investment book in his hand, Kaedon looked up at her late entry with a curious glance. It wasn't like her to stay out well beyond the evening hour without calling to notify him first. That way he would not have a reason to worry.

"Sorry I'm late baby!" Trenika hung her jacket in the coat closet of the corridor and stepped out of her flats to allow her feet to breathe.

"Yep," was Kaedon's only response.

Trenika asked about dinner and Aryanna announced that they had already eaten. Her plate was left in the oven still warming and smelling delicious, which was another thing about Kaedon, the nigga sure knows how to cook too. After stepping behind the sofa and leaning down over the back to give her man a kiss, Trenika asked him what was that he was reading. Kaedon showed her the cover of the book.

"I know what I want to invest in now," he said.

"A truck driver?"

"And studying for my CDL's also," said Kaedon.

"To be a driver as well. Sounds interesting. But I think you need to come with me for a minute." She reached for the book, took it from his hands, marked the page he was on, and set it aside. Then, she took him by the arm and pulled him up.

"Meet me in the art room now," said Trenika.

Kaedon saw it in her eyes, heard it in her voice, that if he didn't get up and come meet her in the art room now, there would be consequences.

For a brief second, Kaedon wondered if this was about him smoking weed in her car earlier today. No. This was something else entirely. So, he got his ass up and went to go see what was going on. In the art room, Trenika was sitting in front of her computer when he entered. She turned her chair fully around to face him with the most earnest look on her beautiful face.

"What's up, bae?" He replied.

"Remember that girl from Friday night at the movies?" Trenika said with a hint of mystery.

He frowned at the thought of the young crazy girl. He was convinced that she was either on drugs or it was just a simple mistaken identity. But for some reason, Kaedon had a feeling that Trenika was about to say something different.

"I remember," he grumbled.

"What if I told you that what she said was true."

"Which part?" He asked.

"About you having a twin brother."

Kaedon didn't answer her right away as he just glared down at her like she was crazy.

"That's straight up bullshit!"

"What if I told you that's why I'm late getting in because I took the time out to go meet him?" she watched as his face changed to several different expressions.

Trenika left knee was bouncing repeatedly. She was obviously nervous, and what she was seeing right now scared her.

With the shake of his head Kaedon said, "I don't got time for you and your bullshit games, Trenika." Then, he turned around and headed for the door.

"You said you'll never turn your back on me again, Kaedon. I need you to listen," she said before reaching around and punching a key on her computer's keypad.

Suddenly, the sound of another man's voice, whose tone was similar to Kaedon's exploded from the computer's Blue Tooth sound system causing Kaedon to halt in step the instant he stepped out of the art room. Kaedon turned at the voice and looked in Trenika's direction. She moved aside so he could look at the computer screen. Kaedon captured by what he was hearing and seeing from the distance, reentered the room and came to rest in front of the computer screen. Professor Zamon Newman was in the middle of teaching a class of History majoring students from his classroom platform. Sometime before returning home, Trenika took out the time to edit the footage and bring Zamon's image up closer. The lecture was only about five minutes, which was enough time to get Kaedon's attention. Then, it switched over to the first encounter between him and Trenika and the root of their conversation.

Kaedon took another step forward as he stared at the now close-up photo of his mysterious twin brother as he listened to the conversation recorded. Trenika looked up at him and sensed the storm raging inside of him. His breathing became heavier and heavier as he glared into the smiling face of the man upon the screen before him. Something in Trenika warned her that he was about to explode any second now. She could see it in the way his eyes glazed over to something very dark and cold and dangerous. And that's when he snapped.

Kaedon growled and drew back and punched the computer screen forcing his hand right through it on impact. Not even the electrical current inside was enough to affect him. Kaedon snorted like a raging bull, his chest heaving up and down, and then he turned around and marched out of the room.

Kaedon wait!" Trenika took off after him as she watched him snatch his car keys and stormed towards the front door.

"Where you going, Daddy?" Aryanna looked up at him from the carpeted floor of the family room.

Kaedon didn't even look her way as he opened the front door and went outside. There was a trail of blood dripping from Kaedon's wounded hand from the floor of the art room all the way to his truck outside.

"Hold on a minute, Kaedon. We need to talk about this!" Trenika caught him just as he opened the driver's door of his truck.

She took him by the arm and to her own shock, Kaedon shoved her away so hard that she tripped over her feet and fell to the ground. This really stunned her. Trenika could not believe what had just happened. Slamming the truck door behind him, Kaedon turned the engine and sped down the driveway into the street. He whipped the big truck correctly in the middle of the street and roared away. Trenika watched helplessly as the truck disappeared up the street and around the corner out of sight, but you could still hear its monster engine in the distance, which probably wasn't too far off from what the rage in Kaedon's heart sounded like.

"Daddy's hurt, Mommy," Aryanna said sadly as she proceeded to use the dish towel from the kitchen to wipe the blood drops from the floor.

She literally had found a way to attain the dish detergent and use it to get up the trail of blood. When Trenika walked back inside the house limping from her hurt knee from the fall on the gravel driveway, she knelt down to help her baby girl clean up the blood. Trenika forced back her tears to keep from crying in front of her daughter.

"Daddy fell and hurt his hand on my computer in the art room." Trenika hated lying to baby girl.

"Then, why didn't he let you fix it for him, Mommy? You did it before when he cut his finger on my bicycle chain." Aryanna was very saddened about the situation.

"Not this time, baby girl."

Trenika wished that she knew but she had to reassure baby girl that he would be okay because the last thing she wanted was for Aryanna to believe that Kaedon and she were not getting along. Not with that being the case, but Aryanna's mindset catches something that her little brain couldn't comprehend.

After they cleaned up the blood and washed up afterwards, Trenika sent baby girl to her room and promised to come by later.

"But I don't wanna go to bed now, Mommy. I need to be up when Daddy gets back. I need to make sure he is alright." Aryanna pouted.

But Trenika wasn't having it, not tonight. Baby girl had school tomorrow and she needed her rest.

"You'll see Daddy in the morning when you get up, baby. Now, get to bed. I'll be there to tuck you in in a minute," she told her from the bathroom.

"I don't need you to tuck me in, Mommy. It's okay. I'm not a baby anymore."

"What?" Trenika spun on her heels.

Aryanna stomped down the hall to her bedroom and shut the door behind her. Instead of going in there to chastise her five year old daughter for being slick out the mouth, Trenika hurried across the hall to her own bedroom. There she looked for her cellphone until she realized it was still in the art room plugged into the laptop computer.

In the art room, Trenika picked up her damaged computer from the floor and sat it back down upon the desktop. Then, she retrieved her phone and hoped like heck it wasn't broken too.

"Where are you, my love?" She whispered as she hit Kaedon's number on speed dial.

No answer.

She tried again and stepped back across the hall to their bedroom. Suddenly, she heard what sounded like Kaedon's cellphone ringing somewhere in the house. Trenika followed the sound of the ringing phone and located it charging up on top of the kitchen counter.

"Ah shit," she muttered in disdain.

"Now what to do?" Thought Trenika as she stared at Kaedon's phone like a sad, lonely puppy.

Chapter 20

Ciera was stretched out in her bed, sound asleep when the sound of her front door being kicked in sent her jolting up and out of bed immediately. Then with the quickness, Cierra opened the drawer of her nightstand, extracted the gun and its full clip, slapped the magazine in, and turned for the door. She did all this in a matter of several seconds before she felt secure.

"CeeCee!" boomed Kaedon's voice that literally shook the quiet house in its wake.

Moving out into the hallway outside her children's rooms, Ciera peeped in at them and only saw Malik sitting up in bed. Tyquan was still in there knocked out cold and hanging halfway off the bed.

"Ciera," Kaedon called out to her from somewhere at the front of the house. "Bring your ass in here!" He demanded, his tone hard as two mountains.

"Go in there with your brotha and stay in the room. Lock the door and remember what I told you about protecting yourself and your brotha."

"Yes, ma'am," came her son's reply.

"Now go!" She whispered.

Malik scrambled out of bed and out of the room into his little brother's. Ciera stood guard as she stared at the mouth of the hallway. Regardless of the fact that it was her brother's voice, Ciera couldn't be too careful and wanted to make sure her sons were secured. By now, Malik had his brother's bedroom window open and ready to escape through it once she gave her call. They were to get out and hide behind the shed of the neighbor's backyard for fifteen minutes before taking the back alley all the way across to Uncle Bud's house. Ciera had them well-trained. That's what being the sister of a well-known gangsta teaches you. Always be on point and never look back.

Without further ado, Ciera marched up the hallway and into the dark living room where she found her brother. The front door was hanging halfway open off its hinges. Ciera frowned and stomped over to the door and forced it back shut into place. Then, she switched on the living room light to take a good look at her obviously upset brother, but the darkness she saw in his eyes and the murderous glare on his face, Ciera had to will herself not to run to him to reassure him her love and protection.

"Why didn't you tell me, CeeCee?" Came the hurt and agony in his voice.

"Why didn't I tell you what, Kaedon?" Ciera pressed the safety button on her gun and sat it on top of the glass table next to the couch she was standing in front of.

No way would she give Kaedon reason to believe that she would use it on him. Sitting straight up in the Bubble 2 single seater chair he was occupying, Kaedon looked across the room at his big sister like he wanted to thrash her.

"Why didn't you tell me that I had a twin brotha? I thought there were no secrets between us. Obviously, there is because I know the truth now," he said.

"Boy, what the hell are you talking about?" Ciera regarded him with a look of dismay. "Are you drunk?"

"When have you ever known me to drink, Ciera? Stop fuckin' trying me before I really snap," he warned.

"I'm not trying you, Kae. I don't know nothing about no damn twin brotha! Where are you getting this from? Who the hell have you been talking to?" Ciera threw caution to the side and moved towards her brother and knelt down in front of Kaedon. "What is going on?"

Kaedon looked her dead in her eyes, searching for any signs of betrayal, dishonesty, but there was neither of them within the hazels of her eyes. Ciera knew nothing and it disturbed him even more to know that she had been betrayed too.

"What's going on, Kae?" She took her brother's hand and felt it shaking.

"It's true, CeeCee," he murmured. "They lied to us. Mama. Grandma Lillie." Kaedon couldn't believe that he was actually saying those words. "Where is your phone?"

Reluctantly, Ciera got up to go to retrieve her phone from the bedroom. In doing so, she checked on the boys and found them both standing before the open window, both looking ready to take flight and get missing. Ciera assured them all was well and for Malik to get back to his room and get to bed. Then, she entered her bedroom to get her phone and meet Kaedon back in the living room. If what her brother had said was really true, then there would be so much anger in her heart for their mother, Grandma Lillie and Uncle Bud, who was the last one left that could shed some light on the situation. She was gonna take it straight to him.

Reentering the living room Kaedon told her to call Trenika and have her send the video she let him see earlier. It didn't take a rocket scientist to sense that Kaedon was avoiding the possibility to talk with his woman.

"What did you do, Kaedon?"

"What?"

When Kaedon looked down at his hand Ciera followed his gaze and gasped. Cakes of blood was all over his hand, his knuckles were bruised and cut all up. Ciera felt her heart burn with fear at what she hoped like hell her little brother didn't do to his woman. Her friend to be exact.

Feeling as though he owed her an explanation, Kaedon told her what went down and that he was sorry for running out on her the way he did.

"You need to apologize to that woman, Kae."

"I will," he promised. "Later."

Ciera made the call, and Trenika answered it on the first ring. She must have been sitting next to the phone or already had it in her possession to answer it so fast.

"Is he there with you now, CeeCee?" Trenika asked.

"Yes," Ciera admitted.

"Can I talk to him?" Trenika sounded so fragile.

That's when she looked at her little brother, and Kaedon stood up and left the room for the bathroom down the hall.

"Right now, isn't a good time for him, sis. Trust me when I tell you this." Ciera had to be straight up with her.

A long paused transpired.

From the other side of the phone, Ciera heard Trenika crying softly and she felt like shit to be in the middle of her sadness. So, before all else ends, she spoke to Trenika on a woman to woman basis and encouraged her that she needed to tighten the fuck up and be strong for her man.

After that, Trenika sent her the recording and Ciera wasted no time reviewing it. In the back of her mind, she wondered why her brother just up and left home to drive all those lonely hours to her in the middle of the night. It was going on 3:00 in the morning and here she was about to have her mind completely blown with a lie that has shaped her life for the past thirty-six years.

As Ciera watched the video, her heart squeezed with burning emotion, Tears spilled from her eyes at the truth of the heaviest betrayal she'd ever had to experience in her life. Moment before the whole entire video had completed, Kaedon returned with his hand cleansed and wrapped tightly. He perched on the arm of the sofa and listened to the last few moments of the conversation between Zamon and Trenika that he never got the chance to even hear. When the video was done, the room was silent as a graveyard. Kaedon looked over at his sister and she just sat there with her face in her hands. No words could describe the type of pain they both were feeling in their hearts at that moment.

The father that Kaedon never got the chance to enjoy died two months after he was born. Now that was even questionable because who's to say that it was his real biological father. Only Ciera has memories of the man she only spent the first six years of her life knowing. The stories Kaedon had been told of the man whose name was Lamar Smith now seemed nonexistent to him now.

"Why would he give a fuck about a man he never ever met?" He thought to himself.

Now Ciera's biological father, whom their mother had betrayed her then husband Lamar with, Kaedon knew personally and couldn't care less about the nigga. It was because of him and Twan he ran down to Miami to build another family of his own and left Ciera the fuck alone. Timothy Crawford was a coward, a drunk, and a poor excuse for a father when he didn't know the first thing about being one. Kaedon's whole life has been nothing but drama after the other. Now, it turns out that his life wasn't really his life because it was supposed to have been spent growing up with his identical twin brother he didn't even know.

"Call Bud," said Kaedon, breaking their silence.

"That's what I was just thinking." Ciera lifted her head, and her eyes were wet with tears and her nose red from the emotional strain.

She called up their Uncle Bud. Kaedon refused to label the man "uncle" what with the lies spiraling around them now. It was until he proved himself worthy before Kaedon could look at him as family. Because he took that family shit seriously, Kaedon's liable to shoot his old ass tonight if he play. Tonight was not for bullshitting. A gangsta's pain was involved.

Chapter 21

Uncle Bud looked every bit of his sixty-two years, and thirty of them were spent smoking a pack of Newports a day, and his love for coke every now and then didn't do him any better. The man eyed Kaedon and Ciera like they were a pair of irritating gnats that keeps flying around his bushy eyebrows. When they came knocking at 3:30 a.m. in the morning, he knew something was terribly wrong. In fact, he knew why they had come at such an hour. He didn't even give either one of them the chance to say anything before he told them both to sit down and listen.

Kaedon had refused to do anything Uncle Bud said and just leaned against the wall nearest Ciera, who indeed had taken her place on the sofa across from her uncle. Ciera was still crying. Then, Uncle Bud lit himself a Newport 100.

"On April 9th, 1991, Kaedon, you was born and birthed from a woman named Moya Moore who had complications during birth and died with both of you boys still in her womb. You were the first baby by four minutes, and then your brotha. That same day, my sista Samantha's child died. She was a girl."

Uncle Bud glanced in the direction of Ciera and saw that she was broken by his words.

"Both Samantha and Lamar no longer could have any more children together due to the damage that child had cause her. That shit almost killed my sista," he said and dropped a tear of his own.

"But Lamar, being the true man that he was learned about you boys' situation and decided to adopt you. Why he didn't just take both of y'all I don't know why, but having you saved my poor sista. But I think his reason was because some family up north had already chosen to take the other child with them," Uncle Bud replied.

"Where was she from?" Asked Kaedon, fuming mad.

"Your biological mama?"

He nodded.

"I'm told she had something like a West Coast accent. I can't tell you much about that. As for your daddy, I don't know who the hell he was neither."

"And I was really born in Cairo, Georgia?"

Uncle Bud nodded. "Only because my sista wanted to protect y'all from the truth…" he paused suddenly, titled his head in that thoughtful way that people do, and bolted from his chair at once. "Goddammit!" He cursed out loud.

"What's wrong?" Ciera stood up with alarm.

"I think I got something!" Uncle Bud said as he rushed out of the room with his face scrunched up, as his cigarette dangled from between his lips.

Watching him leave the room so suddenly, Kaedon turned to his sister with a look of suppressed anger on his face. To hear that his real biological mother had died during childbirth had him all twisted up inside.

"I don't care what the truth is," said Ciera in that stubborn tone of hers. "You're still my little brotha."

It was just what Kaedon needed to hear to move over and sit next to his sister. He tossed his arm over her shoulder and pulled her to him.

"And you'll always be my big sis, CeeCee," said Kaedon and kissed the side of her head.

"No matter what?" She said.

"No matter what."

A minute later, Uncle Bud came huffin' and puffin' along as he gripped the handle of a suitcase with two hands and carried it into the room. Kaedon got up and took the suitcase with one hand and brought it over to where he had just been sitting next to Ciera. Uncle Bud appeared to be exhausted as he dropped down into the chair crookedly and shook out another cigarette.

"That's from all that damn smoking," said Ciera. "Stop it!"

"I will one day," he said.

"When?"

"Never," he said.

Then, he looked over at Kaedon and said, "I think you'll find what you are lookin' for in there. I brought it over from mama's house after she passed. I had totally forgotten Lamar and my sista had buried your mama. They had a small ceremony for her and everythang." Uncle Bud put flame to his Newport.

Right then, Ciera got up and snatched the cigarette from his mouth and reached in his flannel shirt pocket for the pack he had there. Ciera told him no more smoking around her and Uncle Bid threw up his hands in surrender. Meanwhile, Kaedon opened the suitcase and the first thing that his eyes landed on was an old yellowish faded dress. Uncle Bud said it was Moya's favorite dress. Sitting the dress aside, Kaedon reached back inside the suitcase where his eye caught a piece of plastic material. He moved what looked like a folded pair of iron-washed jeans aside and discovered a large Ziploc bag beneath it.

"There you go right there," Uncle Bud stated as he sat at the edge of his seat.

Inside the plastic bag was what appeared to be a billfold wallet and some paper documents. He opened the bag and reached for the wallet first.

"Moya Jhene Moore. Born October 19, 1966. This is a California I.D.," said Kaedon as he held up the old I.D. that too was fading with age.

But not so much that he couldn't identify the address given on the card, and he only could see little of her face.

Kaedon felt his heart skip a beat when he noticed a photo inside one of the side pockets of the wallet. He pulled it out and examined it.

"Lemme see," Ciera leaned over to look at the single photo along with him.

On the photo were three women, one whom Kaedon knew automatically was his mother who was in the middle, with her arms around the shoulders of the other two. But Kaedon wasn't seeing no other face but the beautiful one of his late mother's.

"See if it's something on the back," said Ciera.

When he turned the photo there were only three words written on the back in faded blue ink.

"Me, Sasha, and Amy," he said and continued to stare at his mother's face some more.

"One of them is white," he added.

"They might be friends or something. I know a few tech people who can probably tell me who they are exactly," said Ciera hopefully.

"You do that." Kaedon gave her the photo.

Uncle Bud then spoke on the matter about no one having shown up in Moya's favor after she passed. The little burial ceremony that was taken place, none of her family showed up except for one person who claimed she was Moya's friend.

"Who was she?" Ciera asked.

"Yeah," said Kaedon as he retrieved the four-page document from the plastic bag.

"Her name was Evette Young. Her and Lamar used to go to school together up in Blakely, Georgia. Back then, Evette ran a homeless shelter for women and children. Sure did. I miss ole' Evette with her fast self." He chuckled.

"Is she still living?"

"Your guess is as good as mines, child. But I tell you what, if she is and you find her, tell her I said I still remember that sweet promise," said Uncle Bud.

Ciera didn't dare ask him about that sweet promise for fear of something nasty would be his response. Having seen enough to go on, Kaedon folded the documents he was reading and stuffed them into his back pocket. Then, he replaced what all he removed from the suitcase and locked it shut. Without a word, he stood up with the suitcase in hand and headed for the front door. Ciera followed suit, hurrying to get the door for her brother and thanking their Uncle Bud.

"Hey! My cigarettes!" Uncle Bud called out after his niece before she walked through the door.

"No. Go to bed, Uncle Bud!" She said and slammed the door behind her.

Not being able to go to sleep since the incident with Kaedon's heartbreak, Trenika moped around the house trying to stay calm. After a while, she decided to make herself some hot chocolate. A good cup of that would definitely cheer her up some.

In the kitchen standing before the island counter where she was preparing her drink, something out her peripheral vision caught her attention. When she turned towards the kitchen window, she discovered the flashing of a light coming from the house next door. Trenika stepped in front of the window and to her surprise, it was the strange woman again. But this time the woman made it evident that she wanted to talk.

"What are you saying?" Trenika responded to the woman's frantic hand signals.

Next, the strange woman stopped, seemed thoughtful for a moment, and placed her hands together in a praying sign. Then, she pointed both index fingers at herself and mouthed the word "me."

"You..." Trenika nodded.

The woman then pointed at Trenika and gave her the prayer hands again, then held up the phone sign to her ear before waving both hands back toward herself in a beckoning gesture.

In her own way, Trenika responded back. "You want to use my phone?" She signaled with her hands and the woman nodded her head eagerly.

The woman once again put her finger to her lips in a hush gesture and waved her over to the window. Trenika stared down into the empty sink for a thinking moment, trying to figure out what direction she should take. From what she interpreted from the woman is that she needed to use the phone but to be quiet about it. She must be in some kind of trouble and needed Trenika's help. When Trenika lifted her gaze back up, the woman was holding up prayer hands.

"Hold on," said Trenika with a patient finger, then exited the kitchen for the family room.

Then, she retrieved her cell phone and immediately put it on silent mode. Then, she begin to type in a short message of instructions that she wanted the woman to follow. Two minutes later, Trenika was outside creeping in the shadows towards the kitchen window next door. The woman had the window partially opened up enough to reach a hand out to grab the phone.

"Read the text message I wrote," whispered Trenika.

"You're a lifesaver," she replied softly. "Thank you so much," she ducked back inside the window.

Trenika saluted her and hurried back to her side. Now all she got to do was get back safely and hoped the woman follow the instructions given. Upon entering her home, both Eightball and LuLu stood guarding the front door like two mercenaries.

"It's alright, y'all. I'm back," said Trenika as she stroked both of their heads. Then, she went to retrieve Kaedon's phone where she left it.

A minute later, Trenika was sitting on the foot of her queen-sized bed and dialed the number to her own phone. She waited for the woman to answer, and she did on the third ring.

"Hello?" Came the firm but low voice of the woman.

Trenika could clearly hear what sounded like the shower running in the bathroom on the other end of the phone.

"What's your name?" She asked.

"Jourdan," said the woman. "So, you picked up quickly what I've been wanting to do for so long now. Thank you because I need a friend," she confessed.

"Friends are hard to come by, Jourdan."

"Who're you tellin'!" Jourdan exclaimed. "Trust me. I know."

"So," Trenika sighed as she stared down at her scraped knee from the fall. "What's your story?"

A troubling breath of exasperation came from the woman on the other end of the phone.

"I don't even know where to begin, Trenika.

"Just start with why y'all are always cooped up in that house and not enjoying your freedom."

"Because we are imprisoned, sista."

It was then that the woman named Jourdan admitted that they were in witness protection and the house they were occupying was a safe house. As Trenika listened without cutting in, she learned that the woman's husband, whose name was Al, was a partner in this large law firm out in Chicago. Not only was Al a witness to the CEO of the law firm's acts of corporate tax invasion and multimillion dollar embezzlement, but murder of another partner and money laundering. The CEO whose name was Matthew Hannon, was now detained and facing multiple criminal charges along with his so-called loyal partners of the firm. Apparently, Jourdan's husband was the key witness that could put them all away, which is why the government was protecting him and keeping him hid until the accused has stood trial.

What the woman was telling Trenika was scary. She now understood why they were acting so strange all this time. Trenika couldn't wait to inform Kaedon on what she had just learned.

"Jourdan," Trenika replied. "I feel your pain. But you know you can't just go around telling people stuff like that. It's dangerous, honey."

"I know. All this is just driving me so crazy! I just wish I can go back to how things use to be."

"That life has to be sacrificed for the future of your family now," said Trenika.

"That's what I was told," said Jourdan.

"And please Jourdan. For the sake of my family and yours. Do not use my phone to call anybody back home in Chicago, or anywhere. Please?" Stressed Trenika.

"I won't." Jourdan promised she wouldn't. "You are the only sunshine in my life that I can trust right now," she added evenly.

Trenika nodded. "Then, let's keep it that way."

Chapter 22

Every morning before sunrise, Zamon Newman wakes up and run five miles to start his day. A former track star back in high school and college, it became a morning ritual ever since he could remember. Running was therapeutic to him; it opened up his mind on a greater scale of things. This was his cup of coffee. Also, being the runner that he was, it also was his opportunity to run with a few of his students whom he had bumped into occasionally. He lived in the college housing community where there were constant frat parties, keg parties, all types of activities going on. There was always somebody watching and close by whenever he needed an extra hand.

Zamon had come a long way from where he was raised in the middle-class section of Albany. He doesn't even know what it feels like coming up in the ghetto. The nigga was fed by a silver spoon all his life. But at 5:00 a.m. that morning when he stepped out his front door for this run, he wasn't ready for what happened next. Zamon was stepping down from his front porch when he heard a voice speaking behind him.

"That's one default already," said Kaedon, rising from his sitting position at the other end of the front porch in the shadows. "Not being aware of your surroundings is a total violation."

"To whose standards, Kaedon?" Zamon turned around slowly to face him. "A gangsta's?"

"In general," said Kaedon. "I coulda been anybody, but yet you leave your family at the mercy of a monster. It's a cold world out here, Zamon."

Grudgingly, Zamon climbed the steps back up onto the porch where he came face to face with his twin brother. Even in the dim lit area beneath the moonlight, Zamon could still see the resemblance of the man in front of him. Standing two feet apart from one another. It was though one was staring at the mirror image of the other.

"I may not be a gangsta to your standards, twin brother, but when it comes down to my family I will kill or be killed to protect them," said Zamon, no longer the professor but a man to be respected.

For a long moment, Kaedon just glared at him, the tension between them high.

"Do you want to challenge that theory, Kaedon?" Zamon did not quiver from his twin brother's act of intimidation and stood his ground firmly.

"That's not why I'm here," said Kaedon.

"Then, why are you here?"

"For confirmation."

Zamon said, "You sure picked the perfect time for this shit, Kaedon. But let's get to it. I've been patiently waiting on this opportunity to talk to you."

From there, Zamon welcomed him into his home. To prevent his wife from barging in on them, Zamon decided to conduct the meeting in his home study office. Kaedon asked him did his wife know about him and Zamon professed he had told her about it a week ago. Since learning the truth about who he was and where he came from, Kaedon waited a total of eight days before he was comfortable with meeting his twin brother.

"You want a drink?" Zamon uncapped a bottle of Scotch.

"No. I'm good. That's not my thing."

"Never?" Insisted Zamon.

He poured himself just a shot of whiskey from the modest bar set up he had in the large office space of the study.

"The last time I drank somebody got killed. Since then, I decided to never drink again-ever."

"When was this?"

"I was fifteen at the time." Kaedon spoke as he surveyed the plaques on the wall of Zamon achievements, and even as for of his wife Melody who too was very accomplished and proud of it.

From his perch on the corner of his desk, Zamon watched in silence as Kaedon went about the big room looking and admiring the things he saw. Now that he finally had Kaedon in his presence, observing him, it didn't seem all that bad as he had expected. Kaedon seemed cautious, curious, and calculated in his cool demeanor. It was a list of characteristics that he himself possessed as well.

It was so surreal to have discovered that you have had an identical twin brother after 30 years.

"I heard and watched your video," Kaedon replied.

"You mean the one your wife took upon herself to record without my consent?" He said.

Kaedon ignored the sarcastic tone.

"You know," he began. "I kinda feel the same as you did. I knew there was something missing, but I just couldn't put my finger on it." He took as seat down into a leather wingback chair in front of the large mahogany desk.

"Do you know where we come from?" Zamon wanted to get to the meat of the matter.

"You haven't done any research yourself?" Kaedon asked and his brother shook his head no.

"At least not the root of the matter," he said.

"But you research me?"

Zamon nodded. "And you're quite an interesting read."

Kaedon figured as much. Though he expected a person of his long-lost twin brother's caliber would have jumped headfirst into finding out where he originally came from.

Then again, Kaedon wasn't going to take his word on that just yet. The nigga could be with the bullshit and holding back on information until he got what he can out of him. Kaedon told him what he knew anyway, with hopes that Zamon reveal what he knew.

Later that very same morning, Trenika was getting Aryanna ready for daycare when there was a sound of the doorbell ringing throughout the house. She left Aryanna in her bedroom to finish putting her shoes on while she went to go answer the door.

Trenika peered into the peephole and gasped loudly. Then, she hurried reached for the door handle and opened it immediately. The instant Trenika found herself standing face to face with the person before her, her eyes welled up with tears without warning.

"Those better be happy tears," said Lance, grinning like a hyena.

"They are little brother!" She cried happily. "They are."

When Lance opened out his arms and stepped towards her, out of nowhere came Eightball and bit into his arm with murderous intent.

"No!" Trenika screamed in instant panic and fear and reached for the dog.

LuLu appeared and watched as her brother savagely sunk his teeth into Lance's forearm and was attempting to rip it completely off. The fresh smell of blood was in the air, but LuLu remained humbled, only growling viciously and standing guard like she was trained.

Trenika was having a hard time pulling Eightball off her little brother. It was like pulling a bear off of a deer. Then, all of a sudden two gunshots rang out and Eightball's brains splattered all over the place. Stunned by the act of violence, Trenika looked up and watched as Lance stood over Eightball's body and dumped two more slugs into his body. LuLu snarled up at Lance, but Trenika threw herself on top of the dog and begged her to calm down.

Aryanna was frightened by the blast and hid beneath her bed. But when she heard her mother crying out for Eightball and trying to keep LuLu at bay, baby girl came from beneath the bed and ran toward the front. When she made it to the front door, she watched her mother struggle with LuLu and screaming for her to shut the door.

"Please Ary! Shut the door for Mommy!" Trenika had both hands holding on to LuLu's thick collar and utilizing all her body weight to keep the dog from going after Lance.

Aryanna hurried over to the door and around her mother to do as she was told.

"Eightball…" said Aryanna when she stepped out onto the doorstep in the big puddle of blood.

Closing the door behind her, Aryanna looked out toward the retreating figure of someone she never saw before. Exhausted from wrestling with her dog, Trenika shoved LuLu away and rushed towards the front door where she knew her daughter was. LuLu went about the house barking and tearing up shit, obviously angry about what happened to her brother. The dog was going ballistic. It was clear her head was not in the right place.

Trenika opened the front door just as Lance was spinning out in his rental car from the scene. Her heart went out to her brother as she knew that what had just happened was definitely going to complicate things now.

"Ary," said Trenika, pulling her daughter to her to try and shield her from what was already too late to see.

"Who was that man, Mommy?" Aryanna asked.

Hesitantly, Trenika took a deep steady breath and whispered to her baby girl.

"That was your Uncle Lance. Remember when I told you about your Uncle Lance?"

Baby girl nodded solemnly.

"I remember, Mommy," she said. "And I'll always remember what he did.

Trenika didn't know whether to be worried about what Aryanna just said or just chalk it up as nothing. But one thing was for damn sure and that being Kaedon was about to snap over what happened to Eightball. Now, that was something to worry about.

Chapter 23

When Lance finally emerged from the operation room of the Atlanta Medical Center, his arm was wrapped up in a large bandage. When asked what happened to his arm, all he said was him and his dog had a disagreement. There was no need to go into specifics about where the incident took place and was the animal put down or not; all he wanted was to get medical attention and leave.

Two hours after the incident, Lance was exiting the medical center with a new attitude. Then to his astonishment, there was Trenika waiting for him outside his exit. When their eyes met, Lance saw the sorrow on her face and knew what he had to do. Then once again he opened his arms to her, and Trenika stepped into his embrace.

"I'm sorry, Lance," she cried softly. "I'm sorry for everything. Please forgive me," Trenika pleaded with him as she clung to him for dear life.

Lance kissed the side of her head and told her how much he missed and loved her, and that he apologized for what happened back at the house.

"I'll bury him myself if you want me to," said Lance, knowing how sensitive the subject was to her now that he had taken away something she loved dearly.

"Me and Ary already did that," she said.

"Ary...?" His eyebrows rose up in question.

"Your niece. My daughter," said Trenika. "She's really upset with you, Lance."

"I'll make it up to her."

With a troubling sigh, Trenika thought about how her brother was going to manage that without Aryanna condemning him for what he did earlier. Right then, another person approached them and when Trenika turned towards them to see who it was, she shrieked and tossed her arms around the man standing behind her.

"Benji!" She squealed with sudden happiness as she squeezed her little cousin with everything she got.

Benji, who was just seventeen when Trenika ran away from home. He was twenty-three now and big as an NBA basketball player. This was the only child of her Aunt Wanda, one whom she loved and treated just as equally as her brother. Benji was not the same little boy she once knew though; the young nigga was a straight gangsta through and through.

"Are we gonna stand here all day huggin' and crying and shit?" Said Lance.

Clutching ahold of Benji's hand, Trenika suggested that they go back to the house and chill. But when Lance reminded her about the other dog, and Trenika having seen the damage LuLu had done to her house during her madness, she thought better not to bring her brother anywhere around LuLu.

"I'll lock her up out back then," said Trenika.

Lance didn't look too happy about that and just shrugged.

"Lead the way," he said.

The Lincoln truck pulled up into the driveway of the house and Kaedon got out carrying shopping bags and a smirk on his face. Checking the time on his watch, Kaedon saw that it was just after 1:00. He was feeling alright and had no worries. The next time he and Zamon met, it would be on a flight to California to go look further into where their bloodline came from. He and Zamon had parted ways in good vibes. Everything was kosher. But the moment Kaedon reached the front doorstep and spotted blood stains there, his heart squeezed with panic as he expected, something bad had happened. Immediately, Kaedon opened the door and Lulu suddenly burst through the door outside. One look at the dog and Kaedon automatically knew something was terribly wrong with the way she was acting.

"What's up, girl?" Kaedon called out to Lulu as the dog began looking around everywhere as if searching for something in particular. She was barking like crazy as she ran about the front yard wildly and threateningly. Without further ado, Kaedon entered the house and dropped the shopping bags near the coat closet. He cleared the foyer and turned into the great family room and let out a gasp of total disbelief.

As Kaedon walked around the room, he saw big patches of the sofa torn out, a large dent impression on the wall near the entertainment center, broken glass coffee table, and all other types of mis happenings that he saw. It appeared as though a hurricane had swept through the main room and destroyed the place in its wake.

Quickly, Kaedon went about the house searching for his family and anything else damaged. And there was from the kitchen to the bedroom to the bathroom and the whole house had gone through some type of struggle since he had gone. Back in the family room minutes later, Kaedon scratched his head pondering over what could have gone down. Then, he got on the phone and called his woman. If there was anybody who knew something about what happened, it would be Trenika. Then LuLu came back in the house and went over to him, rubbing her big frame against him and whining like she was heartbroken.

Where the hell is Eightball? Wondered Kaedon when the phone was picked up on the sixth ring.

"Hey, Kae." Came the sullen reply from Trenika.

"I'm at the house," he said. "And I'm not liking what I'm seeing. What is going on?"

Trenika didn't answer right away, she drew a deep breath, and then she said, "There was an incident with Eightball, baby. I tried all I can to stop him."

Kaedon sat down on the ruined sofa. "Where is my dog, Nika?"

"He's dead, Kaedon. I'm sorry," she said.

He closed his eyes. "What happened to him?" Kaedon asked.

Trenika told him what happened from the moment she heard the doorbell ring and her brother standing on their doorstep. Then, when Kaedon heard about what took place after that, anger boiled inside him. At that moment, all he saw was red for Lance.

LuLu came over and laid her head upon his lap. The dog was really traumatized about what she had witnessed happen to Eightball earlier.

"It's all good," said Kaedon as he rubbed the top of LuLu's head. "Where is your brother now?"

"He's with me," she said.

Kaedon said, "Bring him to the house."

"Kae…" Trenika replied. "I don't think that's wise."

"Tenika, trust me," he told her.

No reply.

Without another word, Kaedon disconnected the call and tossed the phone aside. Then, he grabbed both sides of LuLu's head and stared deeply into her golden eyes. There was no words he could say to her to make her understand that he feel her pain. He knows what it's like to lose a brother. It was a loss that will always be etched on his heart.

Chapter 24

Almost a week ago, while he was in the middle of tending to some needed business out in Texas, Lance received a call from his grandma Cora. From that call, Lance learned that somebody named Kaedon had called her house looking for him and had left her with a number to hit him back on.

After wrestling with his brain trying to figure out whether he knew anyone by the name of Kaedon or not, he lost that battle. So, he called Kaedon and spoke with him, and him in return he learned the shocking truth of who he was. The truth about his long lost sister who had run away from home to escape the monster who had destroyed her world. The truth of that same monster stabbing him to death when he went to go rescue his sister. Romell had got the best of him and when Trenika had called him to the house after she had confronted Romell about his devious actions. When Lance arrived, he sent her out to the car to wait for him, but Lance never came back, only Romell emerged from the house, clutching a bloody knife in his hand. That day was the last time Lance saw his big sister. After hearing the story from Kaedon and reliving it all over again, there was no doubt in his mind Kaedon was who he said he was. And then he told Lance how Trenika came into his life and changed his whole world. But Trenika was hurting. She was scared, she was incomplete not having her little brother or Grandma Cora in her life. So, Kaedon made the ultimate decision to call Lance and bring hope into his life by summoning him down to Georgia to finally reunite with his sister.

And now that he was here and have reunited with her, it came with a painful price. Lance didn't expect to get savagely attacked by a beast of a dog. But in his heart of hearts, he would have fought against lions, tigers and bears to get to his sister. He had already killed for her having slain everybody Romell loved dearly in retaliation for what he had done. Lance never stopped searching for Trenika. It was what kept him sane. The mystery, the hopelessness, the belief that he would find her eventually, and now that he had Lance promised her that he would never let anyone else ever hurt her again.

Now that his mission was accomplished, Lance was very anxious about meeting Kaedon face to face. He wasn't afraid or anything, just not with all the bullshit about how Kaedon was probably feeling about him killing his dog, but what the fuck did he expect him to do, to just get eaten to death by that beast? Lance would have done the same exact thing a hundred times if he had to. And then they finally pulled up into the driveway of the house behind Kaedon's truck. From where he sat in the passenger seat, Lance looked towards the front of the house and saw Kaedon sitting on the porch. He looked way bigger than he did in the pictures Trenika showed him earlier. Next to him was LuLu, who looked up at the car and for a brief instant, Lance thought him and the dog locked eyes from the distance. Lance reached beneath his seat for the gun he had there.

Trenika looked over at him and place a hand upon his knee and said, "You want be needing that, Lance."

"Shittin' me I won't," he retorted.

That's when Kaedon rose up to his feet and stepped over to the front door of the house. He opened the door and LuLu got to her feet. The dog took one more glance towards the car and went inside the house.

"Told you," said Trenika when she saw her man shut the door behind the dog.

"That shit don't mean nothing," said Benji.

But Lance didn't say nothing as he watched Kaedon, wondering what was on his mind now that they were here. After closing the door on LuLu, securing her inside, Kaedon then began descending the porch steps moving towards the car. All three car doors opened, and Trenika was the first to get out. Instantly, she moved towards the door of the gate to let herself into the front yard. Without breaking his stride, Kaedon told her to toss him the car keys. Reluctantly, she did as she was told, and Kaedon snatched the keys out of the air swiftly.

"Where are you going?" Trenika asked.

"I got this, Nika. Just chill," he said.

As both Lance and Benji were stepping from around the car, Kaedon told Lance to get back in. Kaedon walked right by Trenika and exited the side gate entrance for the car. He was focused solely on Lance and recognizing the look of pure caution on his face.

"Let's take a ride right quick," Kaedon said to Lance as he pulled open the door to the driver side.

When he noticed Benji head back around the car to get in, Kaedon stopped him right there and told Benji he wasn't included. Benji paused and looked at Kaedon over the roof of the car, then at Lance who nodded at him silently, and screwed up his face at Kaedon before retreating his steps back around the car.

"You got anything on your chest, lil nigga?" Kaedon asked him.

"Let's ride, homie!" Lance interjected.

One long look at the younger one, Kaedon shrugged and got into the car without further issue.

Lance got in next.

"That's my little cousin right there, homie. He's family. He's loyal," he said.

Kaedon started the car and pulled a fat blunt of Kush from his pocket and fired it up. Then, he got into traffic with one thing on his mind, and that was to have a personal heart to heart with his woman's little brother, the man who has come to cause his family pain.

When Kaedon offered Lance the blunt in rotation, he accepted it and took a healthy pull from it.

"I can't be mad at you for what you did to my dog. You wasn't aware of the threat until it was too late," Kaedon replied as he drove. "Every man has the right to protect himself and you did what you had to do. I woulda done the same thing if I was in your shoes. But fuck that though, bro. You hurt my baby girl and for that you know you gotta pay," he said.

Lance glanced over at him.

"Pay a price?"

"Aryanna will have a hard time forgiving you for what you did to Eightball. If you had been anyone else, we would not be having this conversation.

"I told Trenika that I would make it up to her." Lance passed him back the blunt and stared out his side window at the passing traffic.

For a minute there, he thought he was going to have to scrap with Kaedon, but it turned out that he was a man of understanding.

"We'll see about that," said Kaedon.

By now, Kaedon knew Trenika was probably stressing over what was being taken place between them at that moment. But moments before they pulled up, his cousin Naja had hit him up and told him to slide through her spot over on the west side of town. She said that she needed him to check something out and it might be worth his while.

So, on the way there, the two men talked and shared some things with each other that only two gangstas would understand. One being that Lance was nothing like his sister at all, the nigga was one to be respected. Kaedon knew a solid nigga when he saw one and Lance was definitely one that he could see himself bonding with. It had nothing to do with the fact that he was Trenika's brother, the nigga really was a stand-up guy.

Being the good judge of character that he was, Kaedon saw some good things in Lance's future if he was willing to meet the standards that Kaedon would set out for him, but first he needed to see where Lance fit in regarding his true hustle game. When they finally made it to Naja's spot, which was her "Burn One" weed dispensary shop, and saw the familiar Genesis GV8 sitting out front, Kaedon had a feeling this meeting was about to be very interesting one; indeed, because whatever it was that Naja had summoned for, and if Kelly had anything to do with it, it better be worth the risk of dealing with someone of her class and caliber.

"Burn One, huh." Lance grinned over at Kaedon as he read the designer title of the sign about the entrance of the building they were now parked in front of.

"Shit, you're liable to burn more than just one before we leave up outta here." Kaedon opened the door and got out.

"Whose spot is this, homie?" Lance asked.

"My cousin Naja," said Kaedon.

"Aight. Let's see what cuz got going on up in here." Lance was buzzing good from the blunt they had smoked on the way there.

He was more relaxed now that he and Kaedon had gotten an understanding. But he was still on point; his gangsta ready to prove its essence because he was very much aware of how it goes down in Atlanta, which was unknown territory to him.

Kaedon took the lead and entered the weed shop first and headed straight for the front counter where a pretty bad yellow-bone chick sat upon a tall chair smoking on something so potent that its smoke came out in a blueish hue.

"I'm here to see Naja," said Kaedon.

"You must be Kaedon," the yellow-bone replied.

"You must be that yellow rose I'm supposed to see."

She smiled sweetly, her eyes looking Chinese.

"She said that about you too," she said.

"And that is?"

Again, she smiled.

"Really charming. But my name is Mia," she said before stopping over to allow them both entrance behind the counter where there was a door that led to the back of the shop.

Through that very same door was also the large spacious storage room, and way in the back of that room was another door which turned out to be Naja's office. It wasn't a big office, but it was big enough not to feel cramped up within its space.

"Good," said Naja the moment Kaedon knocked and entered the room. "Now, we can get down to business."

Upon his entry, Kaedon spotted Kelly at his left sitting down with her sexy legs crossed while nursing a glass of what he knew was Hennessy because it's the only brown liquor that Naja would allow in her world of pleasures.

"And who might you be?" Naja looked at Lance curiously.

"I'm Lance," he said as he extended his hand.

When Naja took it, Lance brought it up to his lips and kissed the back of her hand. "Nice to meet you, Naja.

"Likewise, Lance," Naja said as she withdrew her hand and glanced over at Kaedon questioningly.

Official was the silent look Kaedon gave his cousin in interpretation of the question her glance beheld. With that notion, Naja poured herself another drink and one for Lance, and then got down to business.

Chapter 25

Now that they were alone, Trenika thought it was the perfect time to sit down and have that talk with her cousin Benji. Meanwhile, Benji was weary of LuLu's watchful eyes as she followed Trenika around the house. You could tell the big dog was sad by the dejected hang of her head. But LuLu couldn't care less about Benji, she wanted Lance, and Lance better know to never come near her again.

"How about a glass of champagne, Benji? You drink bubbly?" Said Trenika, retrieving a bottle of champagne from inside the door of the refrigerator.

"Pour up," Benji replied.

He was sitting on one of the padded kitchen stools next to the island counter. She poured them both a glass of bubbly and took her seat across from him. Trenika would never have thought she would be at this level with her special baby cousin. The last time she saw Benji, he was still in high school aiming to accomplish his dreams of being a great ball player, but all that changed two days before he graduated high school. The day when Trenika ran away from home and his visit to the hospital to see Lance. It was that day when Benji felt like it was his obligation to step up to the plate, and through his love and loyalty to Lance, he went all out for his big cousin like no one else would. In Lance's footsteps, he earned himself a reputation in the streets that shaped his destiny.

As Benji sipped his glass of bubbly, he dwelled on the possibility of telling his cousin the truth, and that's exactly where Trenika's thoughts were. She wanted to know where Benji stood. She didn't want to get into the matter while her brother was around. Lance would have intervened and prevented Benji from pouring his heart out at the risk of Trenika preaching to him to change his life. At least that's what the old Trenika would have done.

"So, what happened?" She asked.

Benji looked across at her. "What you mean by what happened, cuz?"

"To you," she said. "The way you turned out. Obviously, you're a gangsta now, right?"

"It happened that day you ran away and what Romell did to Lance." Benji went on to tell her how he had went after Romell and with the aid of a still injured Lance, killed everything he loved. But catching Romell was out of the question. He had apparently disappeared off the face of the earth. From that moment, all Benji knew was the streets and building a solid name for himself.

"What about Yasmine?" Asked Trenika.

At the mention of Benji's high school sweetheart, all he could do was shake his head. Trenika and Yasmine's aunt Alicia, were also good friends and old schoolmates who was another close friend she missed dearly.

"Yasmine went to the Air Force straight out of high school. We still keep in touch every now and then, but I lost her though, cuz. She didn't approve of the lifestyle I was living back then. I messed up a good thang cuz, but at least not to the point where she wiped her hands clean with me."

"You still love her?"

He nodded. "Always no matter what."

Trenika remembered those sweet occasions when Benji and Yasmine would come home from school to her house. Her Aunt Wanda was very strict about her son dealing with girls. She had always got on his case about allowing his young puppy love to get in the way of his future playing ball. That young girls were nothing but a tease and trouble that could ruin him if he wasn't careful.

So, during most afternoons if he didn't have practice, he would spend much of his time at Trenika's house courting his childhood love. There were a few times when Trenika would walk in on them necking each other while Benji busied himself playing between Yasmine's legs. Trenika remembered the love she saw when the two had looked at each other. Now when she looked at her little cousin and saw the saddened look on his face when she mentioned Yasmine, she wanted to wrap him into her loving arms.

"So, what now?" She replied.

Benji took a swallow of his champagne. "What?"

"Who's the special one now?"

"Nobody. I mean I got a few who keeps me right, but I'm focused on securing the bag. I'm not with all that love shit right now. Maybe later when I've got that bag up, but nothing else matters except the hustle."

"And what is the hustle, Benji? Selling drugs? Robbing people? Because I can tell you now…"

Benji interjected. "I'm past all that, cuz. I've been stopped that shit two years ago. I own my barbershop now, a landscaping business, and some other shit I'm not at liberty to say. But it's not drugs or robbin' niggas! I'm a young boss now. I got my own workers," he said.

"Yet you're still in the streets," she stated.

He nodded. "I am."

"And about Aunt Wanda? I know she's not in agreement with your lifestyle."

"She not," he said. "Mama knows but she can't do nothing about it. I'm too far gone now, cuz. But rest assured she would never have to worry about unpaid bills anymore."

Hearing him out only told Trenika how much shit has changed since she been gone. If she hadn't met Romell then maybe her little cousin wouldn't be a gangsta right now.

Benji would have gone to college and pursued his career with being a great ball player. If she hadn't allowed Romell to come into her life, she would still be home amongst family and friends. The only great thing to ever come out of being with Romell was her beautiful daughter. Aryanna's whole existence came with a painful price and troubling reality that shaped all their lives.

Looking across at her cousin in silent wonder, she was sorry he had turned out the way she wouldn't have imagined in a million years.

"I'm sorry, Benji. For everything," said Trenika.

He shook his head at her, understanding where her words came from.

"You don't have to apologize to me. It's that nigga who should be sorry, cuz. Especially now after I'd found out where he's at. I'ma make sure he doesn't live to see the other side of them gates. I made a vow that I will take his life and by any means necessary I'm gonna see that it's done. No exceptions.

Back in the office where a second round of drinks were poured and Kaedon blowing on some fire weed that Naja dubbed "That ChillMode" the atmosphere was all businesslike and humble. It turned out that Kelly owned two rigs of her own and Naja was trying to convince Kaedon to buy-in and go into partnership with Kelly. But Kaedon only desired partnership with Naja or go independent and do his own thing.

Kaedon didn't want to involve himself in anything that Kelly had going on business wise until he was done with his homework looking into her. Kelly was fresh out the Feds and there was no telling what may become of her. Kelly could still be a major hinderance if she had it in mind to use this opportunity to indulge in something worth worrying about where her loyalty to her man was concerned.

Kaedon wanted a legitimate business. No illegal drug trafficking or anything in that nature. Being the wifey of a well-known drug kingpin, Kelly was not to be trusted until she could prove herself worthy.

"I think Kaedon and I need some time alone to discuss a few things," said Kelly, sitting her drink aside and looking over at Kaedon.

Naja glanced at her cousin. "What's up?"

He said. "It's simple. I wanna invest in my own trucks. If you're not willing to sell me more of those rigs, then I'll take my money elsewhere. I don't want a partnership. I don't want any drama. All I want is to start from scratch and build my way up."

"I can dig it," said Kelly.

"So, we good?" Lance spoke up, still leaning against the door behind them. "Do y'all have an understanding?"

"We do," Kelly replied. "And yes, you can purchase one of my rigs. When do you wanna come by and check them out? My man Reggie will have them available for you whenever you are ready."

"I'll give you a call," Kaedon told her.

"You do that." Kelly downed the rest of her drink and thanked Naja for the hospitality and the opportunity to do business with her.

She shook Kaedon's hand, nodded at Lance, and saw herself out of the room.

A moment later, Lance opened the door and exited the room next. There was no question where he was headed off to and what was on his mind. Having been left alone in the room, Kaedon pushed back his chair to stretch his legs. Kaedon pulled on his blunt of that ChillMode weed and looked across at Naja.

"I thought it would amount to something. When I contacted my nigga Mitch about lookin' into some trucks for me for a good price tag, he told me about Kelly. Apparently, Mitch had been driving for Kelly's old man all this time when I thought he was doing his own thing. She and her people had their hands into all types of shit."

"Who suggested the partnership first, you or her?"

Naja said, "Me. I figured since she was already into the truckin' business that we could utilize her contracts and capitalize from them."

"And there's a possibility that they're moving drugs through her truckin' business also?"

"Yeah. Maybe." Naja shifted in her seat.

"But you still wanted me to partnership with her at the risk of jeopardizing my freedom and my family by getting involved in her business schemes?" Kaedon frowned and sat upright in his chair.

He recognized the look of disdain on her face and said, "Whatever your personal interests are with Kelly just keep that between you and her. I don't know her. She seems cool, but I'm not gonna invest my trust in her."

"I understand cuz," said Naja.

"What all do you know about her beside her being the wife of a Kingpin? How am I supposed to trust that her business is really legit and not a scheme to pick up where her nigga left off? How sure are you that Kelly isn't acting under the influence of the very same nigga that got her fucked up from the jump?" Said Kaedon as he dumped ashes onto the glass bowl ashtray sitting on the corner of the desktop.

"Okay, Kaedon. You win! I like that jazzy bitch. Been wanted to fuck that bitch since the moment I laid eyes on her. I just thought going into business with her would be a good look for both of us."

"I only want the truck, Naja."

"Then we will just get the truck, boo. I'm sorry cuz. I didn't mean to make you uncomfortable."

"We good cuz," he said humbly.

"We good. Now," Naja said with a forming grin, showing all her beautiful shiny teeth. "I'm trying to see what's up with your girl's brotha." She added with the fanning of her hand.

She licked her lips. "Yo boy looks downright tasty," Naja said and Kaedon laughed at her.

"You a freak, cuz!" He said laughing.

"You better know it! I get it from my mama." She snapped her fingers and danced in her chair.

Right then, Kaedon felt the phone buzz in his front pocket and reached in to retrieve it. It was a short text from Trenika telling him that she loved him. He texted her back that he loved her more. From there, Kaedon went to go retrieve Lance and took his leave. But not without copping some of Naja's bestselling weed and products to take back with him. He and Lance still had some understanding to be reached where the welfares if Trenika and Aryanna was concerned.

"I just want my family to be safe and happy," Kaedon told him.

Lance nodded. "That's all I want, brah,"

"Okay." Kaedon left it like that, not worrying about anything else but Lance's word. Because just as sure as he fuck around and bring trouble to their front door, Kaedon would not hesitate crushing his woman's little brother.

Chapter 26

The next three days were spent watching Trenika bond with her brother and little cousin. To Kaedon it was interesting to witness the love and respect the two siblings had for one another. Aryanna was even warming up to her uncle after what took place with Eightball. It was fun to watch Lance bow down to his niece at every turn. Now, he can witness just how persuasive and manipulating a five year old can be when it comes down to her making one pay for the wrong they did.

It was the fifth day since Lance's arrival when the call came in with the information Kaedon had been patiently waiting to receive. Ciera had come through with the information regarding Kaedon and Zamon's estranged family. The night before, Kaedon and his twin brother planned to take that trip out to the West Coast. He and Trenika lay in bed discussing some very important matters.

"I want to go back home," said Trenika after their lovemaking session for the second time that night.

Leaning up onto one elbow and staring down at her, Kaedon said, "You wanna go back home."

"Not to stay baby, I want to see Grandma Cora. I want to introduce her to Ary. I want to see my old girlfriends and visit some of my old favorite spots."

Kaedon didn't reply.

"We can fly out there together on your way to California. Then, on your way back we can meet up there and fly back home. With Romell being locked up and all, I can go back home for a visit. I want to show Ary where I was born and raised. She deserves to know that she has more family out there than just the family she has her with us."

"But you're always worrying about her meeting people and growing attached," he replied.

"That's when she was younger Kaed. She's matured a lot for her age. I want to share this opportunity with her now that we have a chance to."

"Okay," he muttered.

"Can we go?" She said anxiously.

"Yes. But only under one condition," he said.

Trenika then leaned up on her elbow to be at eye level with him. "What?"

Kaedon leaned over to kiss her forehead. "You cannot speak on the situation with Aryanna around. I don't want baby girl overhearing anything about him. I don't want anybody associated with him around my daughter. Please don't let her out of your eyesight for one minute."

"Okay, Okay, Poppa bear!" She reached up to stroke his face. "And I really want you to meet my granny. You will meet my granny!" Trenika demanded.

"I just don't want you to get hurt."

"We won't," said Trenika and kissed his lips. "God doesn't make mistakes, baby."

With that being said, they made passionate love for the third time and went fast asleep. The following morning, they all met up in the kitchen for a healthy breakfast before heading out to the airport. At the airport, both Kaedon and Zamon led Trenika and Aryanna through the building in preparation for their flight out to New Orleans. Their flight was set to take off an hour before the twin brothers. Kaedon was nervous about seeing his family off on a plane without him being there with them.

"We got this," Trenika reassured him when Kaedon began to panic when their flight was ready.

"I can still fly over with y'all and then fly on out to Cali afterwards," said Kaedon.

Trenika patted his chest and said, "God got us, Kaed. Stop worrying so much."

"I can't help it," he said.

"Zamon, come get your brother!" Trenika called out to the other twin before taking a hold of Aryanna and their luggage and headed for their plane.

Kaedon watched them both longingly as they took the path of the walkway toward their plane. Zamon came over and laid a hand on his shoulder. He told Kaedon that he understood how he felt. There has been plenty of times when he had watched his wife board a plane leaving him behind to go visit friends out of the country.

"The first time is always the worst one," said Zamon with a knowledgeable grin.

"How long will we be staying again?"

"As long as it takes for us to get what all we are looking for, Kaedon."

"A day?"

"I doubt it."

"I'm missing them already," said Kaedon.

That's when Zamon looked at his watch and noticed that Trenika and baby girl hadn't been gone five minutes and already Kaedon was losing his grip. With the shake of the head, Zamon led his twin away to go wait for their own flight.

As for Lance and Benji, they decided to drive instead of flying. Plus, they were packing pistols and other illegalities that definitely wasn't allowed on the plane. By the time they get there, Trenika and baby girl should already be situated and happy.

This was Kaedon's first time flying and he hoped like hell it wasn't like how he saw in the movies. In the movies, there was always a serious problem occurring during flight. Either there was a terrorist on the plane, a muthafucker who drunk too many shots of liquor and begin raising hell or just some bullshit occurrence where some technical issue might cause the plane to crash for some reason. Kaedon wasn't on that, and he couldn't stop thinking about either one of those happening. All that gangsta shit he be on and here he was, Kaedon was afraid of flying on a plane.

"Relax," Zamon told him when it was time to finally board the plane. "It's nothing to it, bro."

"That's what your mouth say," Kaedon retorted.

An hour later while thirty thousand feet in the air, Trenika took out her sketch pad and began sketching a pattern that she'd been anxious to do. Next to her at the window seat was Aryanna, tuned into the animated movie she was watching on her tablet. With her Bluetooth earbuds in while listening to her music while she sketched, Trenika was interrupted by a tap on her shoulder. She looked over and met the gaze of an ocean blue eyed woman. The woman that sat right across the aisle from her. The very same one who offered Trenika and baby girl the two vacant seats they were in to sit next to a stranger.

Removing the earbuds from her head, Trenika turned back to the woman and said, "Yes?"

"I apologize for interrupting your flow, but I never did get your name?" Said the woman.

She was white with long auburn hair pulled back in a tight bun. From the casual attire she was wearing, the woman appeared to be someone of class and importance.

"Trenika," she said.

"And I'm Cindy Adams," she said extending her hand in a formal greeting. "So, you're an artist I see. Nice. Is it a hobby or career?"

Trenika didn't really want to be bothered, for her thoughts were elsewhere at that moment.

"It's really both. I'm a professional artist. My thing is really contemporary art and painting, water coloring. A lot of my pieces are displayed in multiple galleries throughout the whole East Coast and more. It's very trying but profiting skill, I'll tell you that much."

"Where can I find some of your work?" Cindy asked, powering on her smartphone.

Trenika shot off a few locations where the woman could find her pieces.

"Interesting," Cindy replied.

Then to her astonishment, Trenika handed over her art portfolio and allowed the woman to review some of her latest material.

"I must say, Trenika, you are very gifted. These pieces are so amazing," she said.

"Thank you," Trenika was humble about it.

She was used to being praised for her work.

"How long have you been an artist?"

"Practically since grade school."

Trenika accepted the portfolio back once Cindy was done with it.

"And where was this? Where is home, if you don't mind my asking?"

With a shrug and a quick glance over at her daughter, Trenika found baby girl sitting there dosing off with the tablet nearly about to slip from her hand. So, she put her own things away and removed the device from the lap of her daughter's. Then, she pulled Aryanna to her where she snuggled halfway onto her lap and rested her head to sleep.

"I'm from New Orleans," said Trenika. "Born and raised until a few years ago."

"Going back home for a visit, huh?"

"Something like that."

"Well, I'm born and raised in New Orleans. Rather you know it or not I was brought up near the Seventh Ward. I'm currently a defense attorney with my own law firm. Talk about trying and all, it's a headache."

"A lawyer from the Seventh Ward. That's a first."

"I am," Cindy blushed.

"And Georgia?"

"A friend of a friend found themselves in trouble and I was persuaded to take it."

"A big case?"

"Murder." Cindy frowned. "But just like you are with your work, I'm damn good at what I do. In my ten-year run, I haven't lost a case yet."

At those words, Trenika wondered if it would be good to take her number just in case. After their flight landed, the two women met inside the airport where Cindy's personal driver awaited her presence. There she decided to exchange numbers with the lawyer.

"You need a ride anywhere, sweety?" Cindy asked after her driver took her luggage.

"I'm good. I have someone coming to pick me up," said Tenika.

No sooner than the words left her mouth did a loud shriek sound off throughout the building. Then, suddenly two women came rushing in Trenika's direction at once. Trenika smiled at her two best friends, Angie and Jhene, as they closed the distance between them and gathered her up in their arms. When Cindy saw this, she couldn't help but smile, knowing how important this moment was for Trenika. She was home. And still, she was scared like hell.

Chapter 27

It was that late afternoon when Kaedon and Zamon found themselves sitting in a small diner off of Melrose Avenue in Los Angeles. While they ate, the two brothers contemplated should they begin their investigation now or wait until morning where they would have the whole day to explore the truth of where their mother is from.

Moya Moore was from Long Beach, California, which was the actual address printed on her identification card. Kaedon was astounded by the fact that his mother grew up in the area where one of his favorite rappers was from. He wondered whether he would actually see Snoop Dogg during his journey. For a fleeting moment, he thought about the classic movie Boyz N Da Hood and wished to go see the area where the film was shot. He wanted to see the house where Ricky and Doughboy grew up in.

"What's on your mental, Kaedon?" Zamon replied.

Snapped out of his reverie, Kaedon looked up across the table at his twin brother. Every time he laid eyes on Zamon the shit just seems so unreal to him. Kaedon didn't know when he would even get used to looking at his brother without feeling strange.

"I wanna go ahead and make that call, brah."

"To who exactly?" Zamon said.

"Either one of them."

Kaedon was referring to Sasha Faye and Amy Dilworth, their mother's two friends from the photo he now had in his front pocket. After a brief moment pondering over the matter, Zamon agreed that he should go for it. Kaedon then washed his food down with his drink and wiped his mouth clean before reaching for his cell phone. Both women's numbers had been previously programmed into his phone. Without thinking twice, he decided on calling Sasha first, since the name was one he was quite familiar with. He had once messed with a chick named Sasha some years ago down in Tampa during one of his business trips.

The phone rang four times before a woman's voice spoke on the other end.

"Hello?"

"Can I speak to Sasha Foye?" He asked cooly, looking across at Zamon in silent focus.

"This is she. May I ask who is calling? Because it's obviously clear you don't know me by using my full name?" She responded on a firm but respectful tone.

"I don't know you. But you once knew my mama, and that's why I'm calling. I need some closure."

"And who's your mother?"

"Moya," he said. "Moya Moore."

A few moments later, Kaedon heard the woman audible gasp came through the phone as the name suddenly registered to her.

"Moya. She and I are best friends. I haven't seen her in over thirty years. And you say you are her son?"

"I am."

A momentary silence fell over the phone.

"Well, I'm here in L.A. and I would like to see you in person. You know to learn about who my mama was and where she came from." Kaedon said.

"You're telling me you don't know where your mother comes from or who she is?"

"I was adopted," said Kaedon.

Zamon winced at the word adopted, as a sense of anger washed over him. When he confronted his parents about the situation, he didn't receive no sustenance from it. They claimed that they didn't even know who his birth mother was.

"And you're speaking of Moya in the past tense? Please don't tell me she's..." Sasha couldn't fix her mouth to even say the word.

"Is it possible we can meet and talk more?"

"Where are you?" She wanted to know.

When Kaedon told her, she then asked him to sit tight, that she was on her way. From there it was a waiting game as both brothers looked at each other in anticipation of what was to finally come out of this situation. This was the moment they been waiting for. The moment of truth.

After being stuck in the house for so long due to the seriousness of their well-beings, Jourdan and her family were now allowed to go out and enjoy what little freedom they had. Having been acting under a new identity that the family could pretty much do normal things like any other normal family. But they weren't any other normal family. They were in protective custody and miserable.

The trial was set in two weeks, and it had them all on edge. But even more serious was the phone call that took place between the safe house guard Nikolai, and whoever he was talking to that Jourdan overheard when he thought no one else was around to hear. Now, scared out of her mind, Jourdan rushed back the kitchen to finish preparing supper.

After a while, Nikolai appeared in the kitchen along with Al, who walked up next to her to inspect what she was doing. The big man sniffed the air and nodded his head in approval of the delicious aromas wafting throughout the room. When he turned toward Al to engage in small talk, Jourdan released a deep breath. She just knew for certain that he was suspicious of her overhearing his phone conversation minutes ago. Next, Jourdan wiped her hands with the dish towel and exited the kitchen for the bathroom. She needed help and the only person she trusted was Trenika.

Inside the bathroom, she locked the door behind her and then unbuttoned her jeans. Jourdan reached down into the front of her underwear for the phone she kept there. There was no way she would just have it sitting around the house or hiding it somewhere at the risk of the guards finding it. By all means, this was their prison and her and her family were the prisoners. Keeping it on her at all times was the best option she had. Not even her husband knew the phone existed. Al wasn't cut and true like she was, so it would be her to hold her family down like a dedicated wife should.

She called Trenika.

"Yes, Jourdan?" I thought we had an understanding about our phone arraignment?" Said Trenika.

"This is urgent, Trenika. I think we're in danger as long as my family is in this house."

"What do you mean?" Trenika sounded baffled.

"I just overheard Nikolai talk on the phone out back with someone named Ricardo. Whoever this Ricardo is had promised Nikolai a half million dollars to '*take care of the situation*'. That was his exact words, Trenika. I think he is planning to do something to Al or worse, to us all. And I'm scared, little sister. What should I do?" She asked Trenika in a whisper, trying her damndest to keep her voice down.

"Where is Nikolai right now?" Trenika asked.

Jourdan told her.

"Okay."

Trenika had to think strategically now because she figured Jourdan, and her family were on borrowed time.

"Okay. What I'm about to suggest you do is risky but given what you just told me you have no other choice."

"I'm listening," Jourdan replied.

"Find something to knock him out with. You'll need something solid and won't break. Don't kill him Jourdan! Just knock him out and tie him up…"

As Jourdan listened, she thought about what she could use to get the job done. There was a variety of things she could use, but it had to fit into what she was in the process of doing at that moment. To save her family, she was even willing to kill the man, but she would avoid doing that for all it was worth.

"Once that is done, give me a call to assure me that you guys are safe. Trust me, they wouldn't expect to find you all there," said Trenika after giving her the game plan to escape the clutches of the enemy.

"I will," Jourdan stood up from where she was sitting on the lid of the toilet.

"Stay focused and be brave, Jourdan."

"Okay."

"Be brave," repeated Trenika.

Be brave. Jourdan told herself after hanging up with Trenika and readying herself for action. A minute later, she was back in the kitchen where she caught Al sneaking tastes of the special sauce she was making to go on top of the lasagna she was cooking. She stepped over and popped him on the hand and ordered him to sit down and be patient.

"You haven't taste nothing yet, Nikolai, until you tasted the sauce she makes with the lasagna," Al said.

He liked to brag about his wife's cooking, having claimed it's one of the reasons he married her. Nikolai only grunted in response as he drank his wine and flipped through the sports section in the local paper. Opening the bottom cabinet beneath the sink and retrieving one of the steel iron pans from there, Jourdan gripped its handle and cast a glance over in Nikolai's direction. The man was totally oblivious to the threat that was about to befall upon him. He had no clue that in the next two minutes he would find himself in a dire situation.

Be brave. Jourdan gripped the pan's iron handle tighter as she stared at the back of the man's wide head. He was busy reading the paper, but not Al, who gazed up at her in silent curiosity as to what such a serious expression on her face meant at that moment. Before she allowed her husband to voice his concerns, Jourdan stepped toward Nikolai and drew back wide. The first bash to the back of the man's head only dazed him, but when Nikolai turned to look up at her she hit him again, this time knocking him out cold. Nikolai sat slumped in his chair slowly tilting sideways until his body banged onto the floor with a solid impact.

"Jourdan!" Al suddenly bolted to his feet, bumping against the kitchen table and spilling wine everywhere. "What have you done?" He bellowed.

"Shut up Al or you'll be next. Now help me find something to tie him up with," said Jourdan.

There was no turning back now. Be brave. Protect her family. That was the only thing that mattered the most to her.

Chapter 28

After hanging up with her friend, Trenika looked up and saw Jhene staring at her from behind the wheel. This was her closest friend, the one she known since the sandbox days. Angie came later in life during their senior year in high school. But both women were important to her and Trenika knew she'd made the right choice coming home. Life just wasn't the same without her two road dawgs.

The questioning look Jhene gave her prompted Trenika to give an explanation regarding the phone call. Trenika told them about Jourdan and her situation.

"I'm just trying to help out a friend. That's all," she said wishing Lisa was there with her too.

"Always the savior," remarked Angie. Big, bold, and beautiful was Angie's existence, with a smooth pecan tan complexion that complimented the brown in her eyes.

"And you're comfortable with them hiding out in your home, Nika? Don't you think that's a little too extreme given the circumstances?" Said Jhene.

"My house is the last place they'll look for them. Like hiding in plain sight. Jourdan is smart, she knows what to do. I trust her." Trenika wondered what Jourdan's method was with taking Nikolai down.

The man gave her the creeps anyway. There was no doubt in her mind that Nikolai would set up a mission for infiltration of the safe house to have Al and his family annihilated. A half million dollars would definitely do it.

"If you say so," said Angie in the backseat with Aryanna. "I hope things work out for her."

They continued to talk and rekindle their friendship after being absent in one another's lives for so many years. When Trenika told them the truth about what happened on that fateful day, it brough instant tears. After the crying subsided, a joyful spirit spread throughout the car when Trenika told them all about her successes.

"You go girl!" Jhene gave her a high five as they neared Grandma Cora's house over near Magnolia territory.

With her friends close to her again, Trenika felt more alive than feeling of this being too good to be true. When they finally pulled up outside Trenika's childhood home, she felt her heart skip a beat. The house she once knew to be of a white and green trimming was now a solid cream-colored foundation that gave off a positive vibe. Although the front lawn looked like it needed a good trim, the residence appeared to be in good standing form.

"You ready for this Tee?" Said Angie.

Trenika shook her head slowly and reached for the door. She exited the car right there at the curb and looked up and down the street. Immediately, past memories of her childhood rip and running this same street came rushing back to her at once. Everything appeared so different but yet the same as she remembered from five years ago. Or had it been longer than that? All she knew was that she was finally home again, and nothing was going to stop her from enjoying the experience.

Then without further ado, Trenika took off running toward the front door of her grandmother's house. She leapt over the steps onto the porch before the front door. Despite the fact that her grandmother lived in a crime-infested area of New Orleans where killings and shootings were the norm, she always kept her door unlocked. Grandma Cora was one of the most favorites on the block. The hood loved and respected her as though they were her own. Trenika reached for the door and to her surprise, it was unlocked just like she figured it would be.

After letting herself in the house, she was hit with the familiar fragrance of lemon Pine Sol and baked cookies, but this day another scent permeated the air. Grandma Cora was busy in the kitchen cooking fried chicken, which was one of her most favorable dishes. Trenika followed her nose, and she entered the kitchen to find her grandmother standing before the stove humming to herself. She leaned against the door jam of the kitchen and watched in silent intrigue.

Grandma Cora was seventy-nine years old and still shapely and rocking a head full of thick black hair sprinkled with a little gray. Her redbone complexion still shone without the blemish and her movements were fluent and natural. Trenika remembered doing the same exact thing when she was just a little girl. She used to stand there watching her grandmother cook all the time. That's how she learned the way to a man's heart, which was through his stomach.

"It smells like love in here," said Trenika.

Grandma Cora stopped humming, paused suddenly, and turned at the voice. The instant she laid eyes on Trenika her hand immediately went to her mouth to stifle a scream. Her big soft brown eyes welled up with tears of shock and happiness. Then, she opened out her arms to her beckoning her granddaughter into her loving embrace.

"My baby has come home," she cried.

Trenika's eyes were spilling with tears too as she stepped into her arms to be gathered in warmth and love and endless care. This was the moment Trenika had dreamed of for so very long.

"Lemme look at you," Grandma Cora stepped back to look her granddaughter up and down. "You're so beautiful, my dear. I just knew you wouldn't up and leave me forever. I taught you the values of love and responsibility. Although you are responsible for your own actions, I knew in my heart that you wouldn't forget where you came from. I dreamed of this day ever since the moment you left. You look good, love. I see that you've been taking good care of yourself. I prayed every chance I get for the Lord to bring you back home to me and He answered my prayers. Yes, He did!"

"Mama…?"

"Yes?"

"The chicken," Trenika replied.

"Oh." Grandma Cora spun on her heels and tended to the frying chicken popping grease from the pan. "Cora don't burn no chicken, right?" She said. "Do I?"

"Never." She grinned.

"Mommy?" Aryanna appeared in the kitchen doorway and Trenika approached her with care.

"Mama. There is someone I want you to meet. My baby girl, Aryanna." Trenika watched as the older woman placed a hand over her heart and said a silent prayer.

"Well, this cause for a celebration. My God has been so gracious to me, and I must celebrate another new life into the world. Hello, Aryanna. Do you like fried chicken, my dear little one?" Grandma Cora turned toward Aryanna.

"With lemon pepper?" Said the child.

"And you know it!" Grandma Cora glowed with love and appreciation and went about her business of preparing a big feast for Trenika's homecoming.

The old lady lived to cook and feed those who desired to eat. Today, she had reason to go that extra mile in showing thanksgiving. Angie big ass found her seat at the table fast.

The second Sasha stepped through the door; Kaedon automatically knew who she was. She was the spitting image if the woman he saw in the photo. Sasha had to be somewhere in her mid-sixties and was looking damn good for her age.

It was obvious that Sasha still considered herself ripe for the picking with the way she was rocking her Bottega Veneta sandals and fitted jeans to show off her voluptuous five-foot seven-inch frame. Quite a few heads turned in her wake as Kaedon raised a hand to acknowledge her presence. When she finally made it to their table, Zamon stood up and pulled out a chair for her to sit down.

"Thank you," she said politely.

"Sasha." Kaedon nodded with a nonchalant shrug. "We appreciate you coming on such a short notice."

"I'd do anything for Moya. She was my friend…My God! I am talking about her in the past tense. Please tell me what is going on with my girl," said Sasha looking very worried all of a sudden.

She looked from one twin to the other and all she could do was shake her head. There was so much of Moya she saw in their features and that reality alone made her heart swell with emotion. Kaedon introduced him and his twin brother. Then, he began to tell her the story about how he came about learning the truth of his existence. Sasha listened without interruption. With every word outpoured from his mouth, she was taken back to the last time she saw her friend. That was a very long time and still to this day Moya's disappearance affected her. After all these years, she never once given up hope that Moya was alive and well. But from the energy she was getting it was evident that her old friend had not survived the storm.

"So, my girl is dead?" Sasha said once Kaedon was done.

"Yes," he nodded.

Then, he materialized with the obituary that was made in honor of her death by his adopted parents.

"She is resting with the angels now."

When Sasha received the obituary, she examined it and cried softly as her heart broke to pieces.

"My girl," she sobbed openly as she brought the obituary to her chest and closed her eyes.

Kaedon shifted in his seat and glanced over at Zamon. Zamon being the gentleman that he was, offered the woman his handkerchief to wipe her eyes.

"Why did Moya ever leave home?" Asked Kaedon.

Reluctantly, Sasha wiped her face to get herself together and said she needed a drink. Without further ado Kaedon signaled the waitress and ordered them all a round of drinks, for him a Mountain Dew if they had any. When the drinks arrived and she had her share enough to go on, Sasha started from the very beginning.

"It started from the moment she allowed Ray Spencer to charm her out of her innocence," she said.

Ray Spencer was a local drug lord whom they all had gone to school together. Since the tenth grade, Ray had pursued Moya to no avail. Moya wasn't into the street dudes; her father wouldn't approve of such things. Being the daddy's girl that she was, Moya focused on her education and later on graduating and attending UCLA to study criminal law. After passing the bar and earning herself a nice spot at a local law firm, Moya was motivated to become the best lawyer that ever came out of Long Beach.

During her second year working for the firm and making a name for herself, Ray appeared and hired her to represent the son of a very close friend of his. By this time, Ray was near Kingpin status in the streets. He was next in line to take the drug trade over and become the man. After several attempts to persuade Moya to take the case, she relented and went for what she knew was the best defense. During the course of her representation, it was all the reason for Ray to stay close to her. Eventually, her feeling became involved, and Ray took advantage of the opportunity to have what he'd been dying to have since high school. But it was only good for so long before Ray's street dealings found its way at her front door. All it took was for Ray's enemies to learn about his shacking up with Moya. One night, her door was kicked in and Moya was kidnapped and used as a tool to get Ray to cough up everything he had.

"Let me guess," said Kaedon. "He didn't do it."

She shook her head.

"He didn't," Sasha replied.

In consequence Moya was beaten and raped and thrown out in the streets left for dead. A week in the hospital and Moya suddenly disappeared on her own free will when she learned that Ray was murdered, and her life could still be in danger.

"When she ran away that was the last day anybody had heard from Moya... Until now that you've came along."

As he took all this in, Kaedon was reminded of Trenika and her situation. Here both women had put their trust in these men only to be betrayed in the end.

"Any idea who our true father is?" Zamon questioned.

"Was it Ray?" Asked Kaedon.

"Or the bastards that raped her?" Zamon said with a hint of malice in his voice.

Sasha shook her head sadly and said she didn't know.

"Maybe it's time for you to talk to Amy."

Zamon perked up.

"Moya other best friend?"

"Her sister," said Sasha. "You're auntie. Amy is your mother's older biological sister. If anybody that could answer the rest of your questions, it would be Amy," she replied.

"Where is Amy?" Kaedon asked.

"At home."

"And that being where exactly?" Zamon wanted to know.

Instead of telling them, Sasha thought it was best to show them. This was the part that she worried about the most, because she and Amy were not close as they once were. Moya's disappearance had changed many lives all those years ago. Two was those of Sasha and Amy, both of whose hearts hadn't been the same since that dark day.

Chapter 29

Crips. That's the first thing Kaedon recognized the instant they entered Long Beach and saw blue attire and blue bandanas hanging and swinging from gangsters ranging from young teenagers on up. This was the notorious stomping grounds of Snoop, Warren G, and Nate Dogg. This was Crips territory. Kaedon watched with an open mind as he drove through the set. In passing, some of the homies gave him a head nod while others just glared and wondered who the fuck he was rolling through their hood. Zamon remained humble as he watched and wondered if coming here was a good idea.

With Sasha car leading the way, they followed in silence as the story of their mother's predicament still left then uneasy and angry all at once. Moya had her whole life ahead of her with being a good criminal lawyer. Her love for her man that wasn't right for her had ruined all that. Instead of facing her problems, she ran away from them. She ran away scared and in need of hope and security. She died alone and with crushed dreams of living a long healthy life. Kaedon wished Ray was alive so they he could face him and look him in the eyes before he blew his brains out just like he planned to do Romell.

After a while, Sasha's car slid over and parked at the curb outside a gated residence on 21st and Lewis. This was the Eastside of Long Beach, the one and only street that Warren G rapped about in his music. Kaedon couldn't believe that he was actually occupying the area where which some of the realest rap MC's grew up.

"This doesn't look good brother," Zamon said as he glanced towards the house they had come to rest at.

Standing out in the front yard and on the front porch of the house were a group of what appeared to be to be Crips hanging about. There were a total of six of them, including a female who were decked out in royal blue clothing and mean mugging them.

"Just stay cool," Kaedon told him.

"I don't know about this," Zamon said as he slowly reached for the door to get out.

"Amy's car is here which means that she's inside," Sasha replied.

She opened the front gate and let herself in as the two brothers followed. Kaedon was far from intimidated by the hard looks he was getting from the homies. He didn't need to match their demeanor, for his presence alone carried an air of gangsterism itself. This was a dog-eat-dog territory and Kaedon knew the dog in him bites just as hard as the others.

"What's going on, fellas?" Sasha acknowledged the four niggas occupying the front porch as she climbed the steps up toward the entrance of the house.

"Hold up, cuz!" Said some tall lanky nigga blocking Kaedon's way from coming onto the porch. "Who you be, cuz?"

"I'm whoever you want me to be, cuz." Kaedon barked back evenly, his posture firm and erect.

That's when one of the two niggas standing in the front yard came over.

"Leave them alone, Von. They're family," said Sasha.

"Family?" Von replied with the screw face, glaring down at Kaedon like he wanted some smoke.

The bigger one confronted Zamon about the shirt he was wearing and told him to dispose of it. Zamon looked over at him then down at his shirt. Sure enough, the muthafucker was wearing a red Polo collar shirt with the big blue Polo horse branded on the front. He was probably the only nigga in Long Beach wearing red. It didn't hit either him or Kaedon until just now that the shirt might pose a problem where they were going.

"No problem," said Zamon.

When he saw his brother making an attempt to remove his shirt, Kaedon intervened. He knew that if they stood a chance of surviving through the moment, they would have to demand their respect or die trying.

"You don't have to do that, bro."

"I say he do, partna," said the big one.

"Or what, cuz?" Kaedon challenged him. "Don't get it twisted, homie. Ain't nothin' pussy right here," he hissed.

"Who is this clown, cuz?" Von turned to Sasha and said.

She couldn't help but stand there and watch what was about to take place. She too knew exactly how Von and his crew rolled and for Kaedon and Zamon to fold under pressure would be the worst thing they could ever do. She saw the fire in Kaedon, and so did Von, whom she knew was very dangerous.

"It's okay, Kae. It's just a shirt," Zamon said as he then pulled the shirt off.

Boogie, the big Crip gangsta that ordered Zamon to remove the shirt, snatched it away from him and threw it onto the ground. Then, he stomped a foot on top of it, snarling up at Kaedon daring him to do something about it.

"That shit makes you gangsta, nigga?" Kaedon said as he knelt down to pick up his brother's shirt. Then, he tossed the shirt onto Boogie's face and followed up with two vicious punches that dropped him instantly. But he didn't stop there, he rushed the other guy beside him and scooped him up in the air before slamming him onto the ground. That's all it took for the rest of the crew to respond and pounce onto Kaedon.

"I don't wanna fight." Zamon backed away fron the stocky built gangsta that advanced on him.

When he was in striking distance, Zamon delivered a lighting speed karate chop blow to his neck and came up with an elbow strike that sent the guy tumbling backwards. Then, he rushed in and dropped him with a front roundhouse kick to the face.

"Told ya!" He said.

Meanwhile, Kaedon was brawling and biting hard like the dog that he was. It took three of them to work him over because two wasn't enough, and even those three were feeling the pressure he applied. Kaedon was a beast when it came down to throwing hands, but after a while the odds against him was getting the best of him.

Zamon dropped another one and dove in to help Kaedon with his surprising but unexpected combat skills. Before long, a deafening blast rang out and everybody stopped and looked up at the person holding the gun.

"What the fuck is going on out here in my damn yard?" Amy bellowed from the front porch, clutching the big .45 caliber in her hand. "And who the hell are you two?"

Sasha stepped forward. "They're with me, sugar. Those are Moya's boys. They came all the way from Georgia to meet you," she said.

"Moya…" Amy whispered softly, staring out after Kaedon and Zamon and recognizing something in them that she hadn't seen in a very long time. Her eyes. They had her sister's eyes. "Where is she? Where is my sister?" She demanded.

Glad to be out the clutches of Nikolai and whatever sinister act he had planned for them; Jourdan was forced to step out of bounds to protect her family. After knocking Nikolai out and leaving him bound in the coat closet, Jourdan snuck her family out the back door of the house and crossed over to the back of Trenika's home. Once there, she dug her fingers into the soil of the flower pot lining the edge of the back porch. Inside the soil was the spare key to the house secured in a small plastic packing bag. The key was used for emergency purposes only, in case Trenika had locked herself out of the house and a spare was needed. Plus, Trenika had already plotted this move ahead of time just in case Jourdan's fears of being detected by the enemy had presented itself.

Trenika was always on point. Her situation concerning Romell and his open threats motivated her to rely on her survival methods. Helping a friend in need of the same predicament was no big deal. Jourdan let herself and her family in through the back door of the house. Having been warned about LuLu who was locked in her room safely, Jourdan made her way about the house situating her family and belongings. Next, she retracked her steps back over to the safe house to retrieve the gun she had taken from Nikolai and his car keys. Jourdan took his car and drove across town and left it in the parking lot of a local library. To get back to the house, she took an Uber car and tipped him handsomely.

Once back in the house, she then sat her family down and explained to them the severity of the matter. That Nikolai was planning to give them up for a hefty price and to escape was their only option. Alex Jr., her ten-year-old son hadn't a care in the world as long as he had his PSP game system to keep him occupied. Thirteen-year-old Donecia was so over this protective custody situation that she was adamant about trying to convince her father to deny testifying against his old colleagues and get back to where their lives were without the strain and stress. She wanted to get back to her girlfriends and flirting with boys at school and being the little spoiled brat that she was.

"Maybe Donecia is right," said Al.

The man hadn't been so scared in his life he thought taking the stand against his old boss and firm partners was just a simple thing. He was now convinced that it was dangerous and doing the right thing had compromised his life in the worst way.

"Do you really want to do that Al?" Jourdan replied.

"Yes!" Al and his daughter said in unison.

Al glanced over at Donecia and smirked.

Jourdan said, "If only you'd thought of this at the beginning, then we wouldn't be going through all this shit. But if you don't testify who's to say that our lives still won't be in danger? All it took was for you to plant that one seed of doubt in their heads. You know too much that could sink their ship. I doubt that Matthew Hannon would just let you slide that easily. We both know how dangerous that man is Al. So, I suggest that you make a decision now what you truly wanna do. We have our children lives at stake here. Their futures depends on what choice you make at this moment. So, sleep on it and we'll talk about it tomorrow."

"Okay," Al said slowly as if he was unsure.

"Good. Now I must go look in the kitchen and see what we have to prep supper with."

Jourdan turned away from them and rubbed a hand across Alex Jr's head on her way out of the family room.

In the kitchen, Jourdan cursed herself for neglecting the dinner she had been preparing next door. The lasagna was turning out to be a successful meal. It was one of Al's favorites, but when trouble showed its face there was no time to think twice. She'd rather be safe than sorry, and thanks to Trenika, she now had safety and shelter for her family.

"After tonight, we gotta get further away from here. Can't overstay our welcome. Let's just be grateful for having friends like Trenika to have our backs," she said to herself.

Then, Jourdan decided on cooking her family some old school southern country grub how Big Momma used to do. Fried pork chops and yellow rice and cream corn and a side of buttermilk biscuits would definitely get the job done right. She was in her element. All was well.

Chapter 30

Amy did have a story to tell once she had commanded the attention of Kaedon and Zamon. Come to find out, she and Moya were the only siblings raised up in a single parent home. Their mother, Gloria Bowman, had died four years after bringing Moya into the world and giving the responsibility to their great Aunt Doll to care for them.

Gloria never married, but the father of Moya and Amy was your practical dead-beat character. He was a poor excuse for a father. Charles Moore was a masonry and brick layer by trade, but his love for alcohol had eventually become the death of him seven years after Gloria's passing. But Amy and Moya had been brought up with endless love and care, so much that Aunt Doll prided herself for the successful, beautiful women they had become.

Amy, a retired elementary school teacher, was forced into the life of crime in order to sustain her loyalty to her sons, Von and Humble. Two young hoodlums who grew up to become well-known street hustlers and gangbangers. Both in their mid and late twenties and no strangers to violence. Kaedon and Zamon found out firsthand today. Now having the knowledge that they were cousins, it still didn't give Kaedon enough reason to just put his guard down just because they were family. He was still willing to bust them fools up some more if they got his timing wrong again, but one thing was for sure, and that being the respect earned between the two twin brothers who had no problem holding their own.

When asked about his true biological father, Kaedon was told that Ray had not been the one.

"Moya told me months after the incident that she thought it was by the men that raped her," said Amy.

She was sitting on a plush brown leather sofa with her baby boy, Von, perched on the arm of the sofa next to her holding an icepack against his right cheek. It was a possibility that Kaedon had fractured his jaw during the brawl.

"Moya was good at math, and she estimated the time frame from the moment the incident occurred to the instant she realized that she was pregnant."

"She hadn't done the deed with Ray for a while prior to the rape incident," Sasha interjected.

"So, our father could be anybody out there?" Said Zamon.

"Or already dead," said Amy. "Because believe me when I tell you the people who was involved or associated with them had gotten taken cared accordingly. Your momma was well loved in the hood and the hood was there for her."

"Tell him about Max, mama," said Humble.

Kaedon glanced from the son over at the mother.

"Who is Max?"

"Max is the son of the friend that Ray had convinced my sister to represent. Come to find out there were some pretty vicious people that didn't want Max to win his case. So, they went after my sister under false pretense of robbing Ray but to scare her out of representing Max. This is what was told to me by my sister when I went to visit her in the hospital. She said that one of the men that raped her threatened to do worse to her if she continued to represent Max. Whatever the situation was between Max and those guys it prompted my sister to lose faith and eventually led her to her death."

Amy reached for her pack of cigarettes and shook out one to light it up.

"Whatever happened to Max?" Zamon asked.

That's when one of the several gangsters occupying the room stepped forward and Kaedon looked up at him. This was the one that never spoken a word since the twins arrived. He was the very same one who drew his weapon and was about to blow Kaedon's whole face off before Amy intervened. Kaedon remembered seeing him with the gun in his hand and wondered if his intentions really was to kill him if Amy hadn't put a stop to the incident.

"This is Max," said Amy.

She beckoned him over to sit on the other side of her.

"Is the nigga mute or something?" Kaedon sized the one named Max up and saw that he was and easy 200 pounds solid.

Max was short and stocky built, clean cut and very well dressed in the latest fashion, but there was a darkness in Max's eyes that he knew all so well. Max was a stone-cold killer.

"While he was awaiting trial on a triple murder that he was being framed for, the person that set him up sent some reinforcers in at him. They beat him and cut his tongue out from his mouth," Amy replied.

"Jesus," Zamon shook his head in disdain.

"This the same case Moya had taken?" Kaedon looked over at Max and he nodded.

"So, you did win the case even after she couldn't continue?"

Once again, the hood takes care of its own. Apparently, Max's father was too much of a coward to go down for the murders and set him up for the fall. But that man got what was coming to him. Max made sure of that, didn't you baby?" Amy reached over and took Max by the hand and squeezed it reassuringly.

"It's a cold, cold world out there," Kaedon remarked the instant his phone buzzed in his front pocket.

When he retrieved the phone, he noticed that it was Trenika calling and rose to his feet.

"I gotta take this call," he said before making his way to the front door and outside into the cool evening breeze.

"I love you, Kae," Trenika said the moment he answered her call.

Kaedon smiled. "I love you too, baby. I take it y'all made a successful trip?"

"We did," Trenika answered.

"Are you okay?"

"Why wouldn't I be? I mean, I was super nervous at first, but once I laid eyes on my girls and Grandma Cora, I was good." Trenika went on to tell him how her journey went from the moment she touched down in New Orleans up until that point.

In exchange, Kaedon shared with her his new experience in California and how much he'd learned so far. From where he stood upon the front porch, Kaedon watched the going on transpiring up and down the street. The area was busy with activity as people roamed the street and hung out in front of their homes and just chilling and maintaining. It reminded Kaedon of back home in Quincy how everybody found this current time of day to hang out and do their thing.

Long Beach was no different from any other hood, just with more Crip gangsters putting on for their hood. This was Kaedon's type of environment for real, being surrounded by a hood full of gangsters was his element.

"So, you're progressing. That's nice. Maybe one day you'll bring me there for a vacation and to meet your family?"

He smirked. "We can definitely do that."

"Minus the fighting and gangbanging part though."

"Of course," he said.

The front door opened, and Von stepped outside onto the porch. He sparked up a fat blunt of weed and moved over to perch on the porch railing. Kaedon said he loved her and to give Aryanna a kiss for him and ended the call with a promise to talk to her again in the morning. After ending the call, he pocketed the phone and turned towards his estranged cousin.

"What's that you burning on, cuz?"

Von reached into his front pocket and tossed a Ziploc bag full of buds. Kaedon opened the bag and sniffed and whistled in result to the potent fragrance the weed gave off within the bag.

"Sour Kush," said Von.

Then, he tossed Kaedon a Philly blunt cigar and told him to roll up his own.

"I don't like to smoke with people, cuz."

Kaedon began to prepare his solo blunt.

"Where are you staying now that you're here? I have a little duck off spot over of the beach front that you and your twin brother can use." Von offered humbly, obviously having trouble talking without experiencing some agony.

"Really? Where is this spot exactly, cuz?" He asked.

"Not far from here. I only use it when I no longer wanna be in the streets. You know, like a place I can go to find a peace of mind. Sometimes this street gets too tiring, and one should always have a safe haven from the rest of the world."

Von climbed down from the railing and came over to sit down next to Kaedon who had taken a seat on the porch steps. Kaedon finished rolling his blunt and passed Von back the bag before putting flame to his creation. He needed the high. A moment later, Kaedon was exhaling weed smoke and embracing the vibe.

"Family is very important to me, Kaedon," said Von.

"Why do you think I'm here, cuz?"

Von nodded. "I see that. But here you'll see that we take the importance of family to a whole nother level. Tomorrow you will meet the rest of us and someone I think you really need to see," he said.

"And who is that?" asked Kaedon.

"Tazzy,"

"Okay, and why would I need to see Tazzy?"

"Because," Von replied before releasing a cloud of smoke in the air. "Tazzy is your sister."

"My sister?"

"Yep. And boy are you gonna be surprised when you finally see her tomorrow," Von said, then jumped up to go approach the group of Crip gangsters that pulled up on the scene in a blue Chevy Monte Carlo at the curb in front of the house. Kaedon watched as Von approached the car and conducted a valid handshake with his crew. Then, one after another more homies showed up and before long there were about fifteen Crips posted up out front.

"My sister," Kaedon repeated to himself as he pondered over the matter of Amy nor Sasha ever mentioning that a sister was even a factor.

Maybe there was a reason why Von told him instead of the others. Kaedon couldn't imagine another woman taking Ciera's place, and if indeed this is true that another sister exists, then Kaedon would just have to respect the game and live with it. Family is very much important to him, too. Family was everything. It's what brought him to that point in the first place. So, before he leave California, he vowed to make a point of proving that same family regardless where he come from he was loyal and true to his own.

Chapter 31

That very same night while preparing her sons for bed, Ciera was interrupted by someone knocking on the door. She kissed six-year-old Tyquan on the top of his head and hurried off to answer the door. On her way there, the knocking turned into banging which brought Ciera to a sudden halt. With a look of contempt on her face, Ciera pondered over the matter of getting her gun before she answered the door. Then, the unmistakable voice that called out to her from the other side made her decide quickly.

Without further ado, Ciera went for the door and unsecured the locks before opening it up.

"What the hell is your problem, Tyreek?" She snapped as her baby daddy brushed by her, entering the house without permission.

She stared back after him and already knew she was about to have to put her hands on this nigga. Tyreek came into the house like a whirlwind, clothes bloody, and tattered, and looking like her already gotten his ass whipped. But through it all Tyreek looked like he was still high as a kite from the last time she laid eyes on him.

"Ty, what have you done?" She entered the living room.

"She made me do it, Ciera," he said pacing the floor and chewing on his bottom lip nervously.

"She?" Ciera could only think about his girlfriend Shon, whom Tyreek had been living with off and on for the past three years.

This was Tyquan's father, the deadbeat Molly head who didn't know what he really wanted out of life. It was known that Tyreek had taken to beating up on all his women. He never put his hands on Ciera because he knew Kaedon will kill his ass. Ciera told him to quiet down because she had just put the boys to bed.

"That bitch had another nigga in the house, Cee. I snapped. I whupped him and her ass up in that bitch."

"But I thought she left your tired ass after you used the light bill money to treat your damn nose with that shit?" Ciera didn't want to enrage him further, but she couldn't help herself; for he needed to see the error of his ways.

"We…" Tyreek stopped pacing the floor and sat down onto the sofa and dropped his head in his bloody hands. "We separated for a little while, Cee. I couldn't take it though. I needed to see her. You know, to apologize and ask her to give me another chance? I still had my key to the house. When I went in there, I opened the door. They both were up in there laid up watching some funny movie. This nigga jumped up and I went for what I knew. Then, Shon jumped in and hit me across the head with a lamp. She busted my shit, Cee. So, I went crazy on her ass and before I knew it, Shon was laid out on the floor unconscious. I think I maybe…" Tyreek paused again and looked up at the sudden flashing lights outside the front window.

"Tyreek, what did you do to that woman?" Ciera was beginning to panic right along with him when she noticed the flashing lights going on out front.

Tyreek shot up to his feet and ran over to the window and peered through the window curtains. A loud gasp of fear exploded from him when he saw two police cars out front before the house. They had come for him, but how did they know he was there? Was Shon actually dead? He had blacked out in a dark rage when Shon hit him with that lamp. He left both of them stretched out on the bedroom floor. Tyreek wasn't sure whether he had killed them both or not.

After looking out the window and seeing a third police cruiser pull up on the scene, Ciera was convinced that he had done something terribly wrong.

"We not fixing to do this, Ty. Whatever you did to those people, your ass is going down for it. You are not gonna bring this foolishness to my house. Your son is in the back room. He doesn't deserve to see this, Ty. I can't allow you to do this to us," said Ciera.

"Do what?" Tyreek fiend dumbfounded.

"Whatever you did to get here, nigga. You need to get up out of here," she ordered him.

Ciera glared at him while pointing towards the front door. She saw the look of fright in his eyes at the prospect of going to jail. At that moment, Tyreek appeared to look helpless and hopeless, knowing what he did had put him in a critical situation.

"I can't go to jail," said Tyreek.

"Then, where are you going Ty?" Ciera questioned him.

He paused to think for a moment. "Can I see my son before I go?" Tyreek replied.

"Go where? No. If you're not going to jail, then where the hell else are you going?" Ciera hoped he wasn't thinking about going all out and making them people kill him. Just the thought of him getting gunned down in front of her and her children brought a cold shiver running up her spine.

For a long moment, Tyreek just stood there staring down at the floor as if in deep thought.

"Tyreek!" Ciera hissed at him and covered her mouth with both hands when there was a knock at the front door.

That was the police coming to get Tyreek. Tyreek looked from her to the front door and suddenly it dawned on Ciera that she couldn't let nothing happen to him. No matter how much she disliked her son's father, she couldn't just stand there and watch him go down like this.

"I can't go to jail, Cee. I can't," he whined.

"Not tonight. You're not stupid!" Ciera approached him and began shoving him toward the back of the house. In passing, she saw that Malik and Tyquan were peeping out of their bedroom doors at what was going on. She told them both to shut their doors and stay put. They did as they were told, and Ciera continued to push Tyreek toward the back door.

"What're you doing, Ciera?" Tyreek asked.

"I'm saving your dumbass life, you idiot! Go through the back and cross over to Pumpkin's backyard and go straight to that place we used to go for a picnic. Stay there until you hear from me, Ty. Okay? Now go!" Ciera opened the back door and shoved him out into the darkness of the night.

"Thank you, Cee." Tyreek leaned in to kiss her cheek and got fire slapped from his face.

"Get the fuck away from my damn house, fool!" Ciera shut the door on him and locked it.

Her heart was racing as she willed her surging adrenaline to subside at least just a little. The banging on the front door brought her out of her daze and Ciera growled like an angry pitbull. If there was one thing she hated, it was someone banging on her front door like they didn't have no damn sense. So, she marched back towards the front of the house to give them a verbal thrashing.

By now, Tyreek better be doing what was best for him and putting distance between him and his fate. No sooner than the thought crossed her mind did two gunshots rang out somewhere outside close by. Instantly, a deep grip of burning fear squeezed her heart as she wondered if those shots were meant for Tyreek.

Chapter 32

Trenika was the first to wake up that next morning after a long night with family and friends. Even Grandma Cora stayed up all the way until the wee hours entertaining her company. The celebration of Trenika's homecoming had lasted all the way till about 3:00a.m. but the few hours of rest that she did get was enough for her. Trenika got up and began cooking breakfast for everybody. She knew her grandmother was going to chastise her about invading her kitchen. This was her way of showing Grandma Cora that she too was still sharp in her culinary arts.

Grandma Cora was the next to arise as she came into the kitchen to find her granddaughter knee deep in cooking. Trenika served the older woman her cup of Maxwell coffee and proceeded to continue her task. All Cora could do was sit at her kitchen table and admire her baby girl. She had a pleased look on her beautiful face while sipping her coffee and relishing the aromas floating about the kitchen.

Angie was the next one to arrive and sat down at the table to engage in conversation with Grandma Cora. About fifteen minutes later, Jhene appeared looking sleepy but very alert. She announced that she had to leave for work and hugged and kissed them all before taking her leave. Jhene promised she would stop by on her lunch break and headed out.

Also present was Trenika's cousin Davida and Rhonda, her gay friend Pooh Baby, and Shenita, her other friend from childhood, and the sister of another well-known gangsta.

One after the other, they all arrived into the kitchen at the smell of bacon, cheese grits, fried potatoes, and crispy toast with butter and jelly. Trenika had come and did her thing; she had everybody anticipating filling their bellies with delicious grub. There wasn't even enough seats at the table but there damn sure were enough plates.

"Can I take mine on the go?" Said Davida, a plump cocoa skin complexion female who reminded you of Lizzo. She was the doctor in the family and quite successful in her hand with counseling children with mental behaviors.

"I must get home and get to work myself," she added.

"On a Saturday, Davida?" Trenika asked.

The two were just a few years apart with Davida being the oldest. When Trenika got ghost years ago, Davida was living down in Alabama with her husband of ten years before things got bad and she returned back to New Orleans two years ago.

"I'm not leaving till I get my plate too, girl" This came from Pooh Baby, who also worked at the local clothing store for a living.

He was also a booster and very good at what he do. Pooh Baby was so good that he used all his stolen goods to open up his own shop withing the clothing store he manages.

"My dear, I have some paper plates up in the cabinet over there," Grandma Cora pointed, and Pooh Baby went over to go retrieve them for himself.

Before long, everyone had gone except Rhonda and Angie and Shenita, who was the youngest of them all. Aryanna arrived and commanded their attention and had everybody practically leaning onto her every word.

After eating breakfast and cleaning up after themselves, Trenika said she wanted to go out on the town. It was still early but she wanted to go sightseeing. She didn't want to wait. She was finally home again, and Trenika needed to get out and see what all she had missed over the years. Most of all, she wanted to go visit her mother's grave and give her flowers. She'd usually do it on her mother's birthday and the anniversary of her passing. It was long overdue that she does so.

"But first there's somebody that I need to see before we do anything else," said Trenika, leading the way outside.

"I already know who that is," said Angie.

"Who?" Trenika glanced over the roof of the SUV at her friend.

Angie said, "Ms. Anderson from our Social Studies class."

She and Trenika had shared homeroom class together in high school where Ms. Millie Anderson were their homeroom teacher. Trenika smiled at her friend knowingly. She was right; indeed, it was their former teacher Trenika wanted to see. It was Ms. Anderson who was there for her during some of the most critical moments in her life. She was there when Trenika broke her virginity and was too scared to tell her parents. She was there the day Trenika got jumped by two girls behind the gym and busted up bad. She was the ear whenever Trenika wanted to pour her heart out. It was even Ms. Anderson who encouraged her to put in for college. The woman had a sweet spot in Trenika's heart, and she wanted to give her reason to smile again.

Her, Aryanna, Rhonda, and Angie, along with Shenita, piled up into Rhonda's Toyota Venza and headed out into town. The first order of business was to visit Ms. Anderson and then Trenika's mother's grave. Then, from there it was all out sightseeing and enjoying the love and company of loved ones.

It wasn't until that very morning did Kaedon learn all about who Tammy "Tazzy" Holland was. Tazzy was the bastard daughter of Victor "Smoke" Holland, the very same muthafucker who was penalized by death in his involvement with raping Moya Moore all those years ago. Come to find out it was Jermaine Phillips, which was Max's father, whom some Long Beach homies ran down on and tortured him to death. They made Jermaine reveal the perpetrators whom he sent to harm Moya the way he did. It turns out that Smoke was one of her assailants. Smoke eventually died in the worst way for his actions.

During that time all those years ago, Smoke had had a daughter by the name of Tammy. The nickname Tazzy only came later on in life when she began living a lifestyle that what was left of her family attempted to shelter her away from. Tazzy was six years old when her father died. That made her thirty-seven now, but when asked about her current lifestyle, Von wasn't shy about describing her way of life. From his description, Tazzy had turned out to be a gangsta, one of the most respected divas in the game. A Crip member she was, only because the majority of her family were affiliated, but she pretty much was the solo type having proven at a young age that she could handle her own. It was said that Tazzy was more gangsta than most niggas who proclaimed to be. Hearing this only made Kaedon want to meet her more.

Zamon was sickened by the knowledge of Tazzy being a female gangsta and what this notion may represent. He didn't care for meeting Tazzy but knew he had no choice. As for Von and his situation, Kaedon had misguided him by how he presented himself the day before. He was under the impression that Von was your average young black nigga who thought he was bad and wouldn't account for nothing in life. Your typical wannabe thug who seeks attention and folds under pressure when he didn't have a crew to back him up. But little did Kaedon know; Von had been more than what meets the eye. Vonte Morris had been a high school graduate who attended college on a basketball scholarship, but that didn't last long. Von was shot four times in his freshman year by a crew of Bloods who'd mistaken him for someone else. Those four bullets changed his life and led him to the life of crime. Though he did utilize his intellectual to benefit from his marks and capitalized from their losses.

Today Von was a proud owner of a record label, barbershop, a used car lot, and even retailing. He had two cars, a bike, a condo downtown, and two other homes that he rarely occupied. Von wasn't just your average gangsta, the nigga had a head on his shoulders. His only problem was showboating and an attention seeker, but Von was also a killer. He wasn't no coward from a long shot.

That morning, Von treated the two brothers out to breakfast at an L.A. restaurant named Craig's that one of Von's sidechicks worked. Zamon professed that this was also a place he had visited when he'd come to California several years ago. He claimed that he'd eaten at Craig's twice before and it was quite pleasant on both occasions.

"Tell me more about Tazzy," said Kaedon after they ordered breakfast, and their food arrived.

Von was happy to oblige. "Just know that she isn't the type of bitch that'll go for anything, cuz. Baby girl is really up-up right now. All that blood money she'd accumulated over the years, Tazzy invested it in a law firm and even has stocks in a couple banks in the city. Cuz play for keeps and she knows how to utilize her resources."

"You mean to tell me she has her own law firm? With lawyers and everythang?" Kaedon was astounded by this revelation, and its coincidence that his mother had been a lawyer made him wonder if there was any relation to that.

"The nigga she was fuckin' with some years ago had a little sister who had dreams of being a lawyer. So Tazzy paid her way through law school and built her a law firm. She somehow persuaded a couple well experienced lawyers from other firms to join her mission. Your girl is smart, she knows how to make things happen. I respect her totally." Von had nothing but good to say about her and this too made Kaedon even more anxious to meet her.

"Fuck it. Let's go. I wanna get this shit over with," said Kaedon wiping his mouth with a napkin.

"But we just sat down," Zamon replied, his fork of food halfway toward his mouth.

Kaedon stood up.

"Bring it with you. I don't care. I'm ready to meet this Tazzy individual.

Von was all for it.

"Okay. Go get the car ready while I finish up here."

When Zamon said he enjoyed the food here, he wasn't playing no games. He stuffed his face with his food as quickly as he could while Von went to get the car. When the car horn blared outside minutes later, he got up, peeled off a few bills to tip the waitress, and exited the restaurant feeling quite pleased with himself. All Kaedon could do was shake his head as he rode shotgun in Von's Benz truck. He was beginning to like his twin brother but sometimes Zamon could really be a pain in the ass.

Back on the road, Von sparked up some of that Cali bud and cranked up some gangsta music. It was then that Kaedon received the text message from his sister telling him to call her. He called her without hesitation and what he learned from her about what took place last night was enough to make him worry.

"Is she dead?" Asked Kaedon.

He knew Shon well; she was friends with one of his old side pieces.

"Damn near," said Ciera. "That stupid muthafucker done cave the girl whole face in."

"Where is he now?"

"I can't say right now. Kae," she said.

He heard her loud and clear and understood the meaning from which the tone she had used. There was no question in his mind that Ciera had somehow played a part in Tyreek not being arrested last night. After all the shit that nigga took her through over the years, she still proved that she was loyal. Kaedon doubted very much that Tyreek would notice such things and not truly appreciate her loyalty to him the same way she would. Niggas like Tyreek deserved to get everything that come to him, even the consequences when he fucks up. If it was up to Kaedon, the nigga would have been dead.

"You just make sure you cover your tracks sis," Kaedon warned her.

"Little brotha, I'm not new to this. I'm true to this," she retorted and that made him smile.

"No doubt," he replied humbly. "No doubt at all."

Chapter 33

There was silence as their hearts pounded with increased frequency as the absolute enormity of the situation settled down on them like a stone lid of a crypt. Everybody in the truck held their breaths as they stared out the window at what was taking place before their eyes. The last thing either one of them expected to see was Tazzy Holland with a Colt Python .357 Magnum pressed against the face of another nigga in broad daylight in front of a block full of witnesses. Obviously from the looks of the situation the confrontation was between her and another street hustler. There were a total of nine people occupying the street corner and seven of them were donned in blue attire.

Von had pulled up on the scene of a Compton neighborhood block of East 120th Street, which was Tazzy's territory and that of her gangsta's Crip set. If there was one place one could find Tazzy it would be in Compton. The bitch bled, sweat, and cried Compton on an everyday basis. This was her home and if one did not know, she wouldn't have a problem making you out of a believer.

Tazzy, who stood firmly of five foot eight and with the skin tone of a caramel hue, rocked shoulder length dreadlocks that were loose and crinkly as though they had recently been taken out of a braided pattern. She was dressed in a pair of $590 Gucci sneakers and Levi's vintage jeans that seemed to hug her perfectly round bubble butt to perfection. On her face was also a pair of Anthony Vaccarello sunglasses. Even if her attire didn't pronounce her gangsta, the act she was presenting damn sure was getting the job done.

The house in which Tazzy lived was on 137th Street, across the street from a chicken joint where she still bought the 3-piece meal with fries and a lemonade. Von only took this route first because it gave him opportunity to check this young redbone bitch he'd been smashing on the low. But here it was, he had driven up on a possible murder scene if he didn't intervene. As if reading his thoughts, Kaedon opened the door and got out of the truck.

"Cuz, you don't wanna do that!" Von called out after Kaedon and dreaded what might happen next.

He then turned around and looked at Zamon in the backseat.

"What's wrong with him, cuz! He must got a death wish or something. You need to check your brother, homie."

"I'm not going out there," Zamon replied.

Sucking his teeth in aggravation, Von put the truck in park and got out next. He couldn't believe Kaedon was actually walking into a lion's den at the risk of getting himself killed without question. One thing he had to say about his cousin is that the muthafucker had big nuts. Kaedon was fearless as they come.

"Tazzy," Kaedon said as he approached the street corner where which some straightening was being taken place.

Suddenly, more automatic weapons were drawn as all eyes turned in his direction. Two of the crew members broke away from the group with their guns trained on Kaedon. He raised his hands in a peace gesture and said that he was Tazzy's brother and wanted to finally meet her. The instant those words left his mouth, Tazzy dropped her gun from the other guy's face and stepped away. Then, she gave a head nod that released the fury of three of her men to administer on the lone hustler. She didn't even wait up to observe the beatdown. Tazzy turned and headed in the direction of

Kaedon who now stood blocked by two of her soldiers at gunpoint. She looked past them at Von and frowned up her face at him.

"You know this clown, Taz?" said one of the loyal goons clutching a big Glock .20 at ready.

"Stand down, Lump. Spook. Chill, I got this," Tazzy said and slowly but surely the two goons lowered their guns, but didn't tuck them away.

She then walked up to Kaedon standing there on the sidewalk looking totally unaffected by the odds. Automatically, she knew this wasn't no ordinary nigga and seeing this left her very intrigued.

"It's all good, cuz," Von said as he came to rest amongst them. "The homie didn't mean no harm."

"I know, Von. I spoke with Pierre this morning. He laced my Chucks up on the situation. I just never gotten around to making my presence known. However," Tazzy turned from Von and looked Kaedon directly in his eyes. "You must be Kaedon," she said.

"In the flesh," he answered.

She smiled, showcasing a bottom row of platinum teeth with white diamonds encrusted into them. She had a beautiful smile and Kaedon had to remind himself that this was his half-sister, that shared the same bloodline.

"I've heard a lot about you, Kaedon. Where's your other half?"

"Back in the truck observing the scene."

"Hmph. As he should be. I hear. No disrespect, but I don't take too kindly with chumps like him."

"You better watch your mouth about my brotha," Kaedon glared holding her gaze intensely. "Zamon is just as loyal and devoted as any of us; he just not accustomed to the type of lifestyle we live," he stated in defense of his twin.

"And what type of lifestyle is that, may I ask?"

"The life of a gangsta," he said.

Spook chuckled at that, and Kaedon looked over at him as if to challenge him. Spook took on his mean mug again and shrugged with nonchalance. Behind, the three Crip homies had thrashed the hustler something viciously and left him right there on the corner bleeding profusely and writhing in pain and agony.

"C'mon Kaedon. Let's take a walk?" Tazzy tucked her pistol behind her and beckoned Kaedon to walk with her.

When the two goons made a move to follow, she shook her head no and they went the opposite direction. Von was left looking left out so he trekked back over to the truck.

"So," Tazzy replied as they began to walk along the sidewalk side by side. "What do you think so far?"

Kaedon glanced over at her.

"About you? I'm intrigued. I see you're about your issue. But what matters most is us getting to know each other. I came here to learn about my family that never existed to me until now. I don't care about what the fuck you do or how you do it. Just as long as you keep it G with me then we good. The only thang I care about right now is you, Tazzy. I'm told you are my sista, and I can spot the mirror resemblance, so I'ma need you to help me make this shit work. I refuse to leave here without being satisfied that my journey was worth the risk," he said.

"Are you always so damn serious, Kaedon?"

"Always," he said. "I've been through a lot coming up."

"And so have I," Tazzy said.

Kaedon nodded. "Then let's go somewhere where you, me and Zamon can build. We need this shit for real, Tazzy. We've been lost for too long as it is," he said.

"Anywhere?" Tazzy halted.

"What do you have in mind, sis?" He stopped short.

Tazzy smiled and told him that she knew a place that they could go and build.

After spending a couple hours with Ms. Anderson and since it was approaching noon, the girls agreed to eat out at a local Taco Bell joint since it was Aryanna's favorite place. The girl loves herself some tacos and Shenita was down with it as well. She used to work at Taco Bell and still had a little pull there with the manager.

Trenika and her crew went in and claimed themselves a table booth and got their grub on. Afterwards, the girls rode around the city until Trenika built up the courage to visit her mother's grave. She spent about an hour there cleaning around the gravesite and placed a fresh dozen of rosed around the headstone. She talked to her mother and cried and lastly introduced her to her granddaughter Aryanna who only just stood there transfixed and trying to understand the situation. From there, Trenika wanted to go back home to be with her grandmother. She needed to be around the only other woman who given her life true purpose.

Grandma Cora had expected them all to be back for the lunch hour just as Davida and Jhene had, so the old lady had fixed a platter of various sandwiches and baked cookies. To tell the old lady they had eaten out at Taco Bell would be insult to her pride. So, they all stuffed themselves with sandwiches and cookies and hoped like hell Aryanna didn't spill the beans. Baby girl was very outspoken and had a habit of saying things that shouldn't be said. To spare old Cora injury to her feelings was the best option.

The house was lively and filled with love and laughter as they all sat cozy in the big living room, but suddenly their curiosity got the best of them when there was a knock at the door. When Jhene went to go answer it, she returned a minute later with a beautiful flower in her hand, but it's who she had following behind her that stole the breath of Trenika for the moment she laid eyes on him her heart fluttered.

"Josh!" Davida said joyously and glanced at Trenika.

Grandma Cora beamed up at the man standing before them and stood up to hug him.

"Well, isn't this a wonderful surprise! Another one of my babies had finally come home."

Sly looks in Trenika's direction made her feel as though she was put on the spot with Josh's sudden presence. She watched as he handed each woman in the room a flower, two to Aryanna, and then Trenika was last to accept her flower with grace. She looked up at Josh standing there in his U.S. Marine Corps uniform, handsome as ever and great as any Greek god. Joshua Freeman, Trenika's childhood love and high school sweetheart, the very same person who never denied her anything, but she denied him, on graduation night, refusing to settle a life with him and going off to college. Josh wanted to follow in his father's footsteps of joining the Marines, but Trenika didn't want that distant love; she needed someone hands on and a love to lean on. Their futures were headed in two directions and Trenika had only seen him twice in the last sixteen years since graduation night.

Now, here he was again for the third time looking good and making her heart race.

"Trenika," Josh extended his hand and hesitantly, she reached up and took it. When he pulled her up to her feet into his strong embrace, Trenika thought she would pass out.

"I've missed you so much, my love. How are you?" He whispered into her ear.

"I'm very good, Josh. And yourself?"

"I'm better now that I have you here," he said.

Trenika didn't know whether to accept that statement or beware of the meaning for which he intended. Once look into his eyes and she was reminded of the boy she had always loved and hurt at the end. The boy who now looked at her with endless love.

Chapter 34

Trenika watched and waited for the time to come when Josh decided to have his one on one with her. Since they were in sixth grade, it had always been Josh, the boy who lived just up the street. The very same boy who gave her first kiss, her first hero, the object that always left Jhene envy of their relationship growing up. The two used to war for Trenika's attention. Back then, everyone had predicted that Trenika and Josh would marry one day. Just thinking about those days made Trenika realize just how wrong they all had been. Every other relationship with others after Josh didn't amount to much of anything. They had been Cameron Taylor from across the tracks, Cedric Murphy the show promoter, Elijah Herring out of the Ninth Ward, and then Romell, the worst person she had ever met. Throughout all the men, she dealt with previously of committing to Romell, when he crushed her it was Josh whom her heart had cried out for. The same Josh she crushed, but knew without a doubt he would have come to her rescue if she had reached out to him. That was how much Trenika was aware of the love. Josh still had for her regardless of what took place on graduation night. Josh would have come for her. Josh would have secured her broken heart, and Josh wouldn't have let her go as long as she was willing.

And this day, when Josh finally suggested that they go outside and talk; Trenika didn't want to take that chance, but she got up and followed him outside not sure how this meeting would turn with the way her heart was forming. Once outside, Josh took her by the hand and helped her down the porch steps. Always have been the gentleman toward her. Just touching him again sent an electric current through her and Trenika knew she couldn't let that happen too many times.

"Mom told me about what happened," said Josh, gesturing for the wooden picnic table that was in the front yard.

Trenika sat down and he took a seat across from her, setting his arms down on the table in front of him.

"She didn't go into detail what actually happened between you and Romell. Just that you guys had gone through something that scared you to the point that you ran away from home. But what I'm trying to understand is what could Romell have possibly done to get his family murdered in your honor and cause you to run away?" He asked.

Trenika shook her head sadly.

"Josh…" She began.

"You don't wanna talk about it? I get it." Josh reached across the table to take her hand.

"That man…Romell did the worst thing to me that anyone could ever do to a person," she said.

"Cheat?" He replied.

"Worse than that, Josh."

Josh was about to ask what but was interrupted by the honk of a car horn as it drove by. It was Josh's mother, Heather, driving by to get back to work at the hospital. He waved a hand in her wake and turned back to the woman in front of him.

"Talk to me, Tee. I need to know so I can try to understand your pain."

"You'll never understand this pain I have, Josh. I wouldn't wish this on my worst enemy," she stated emotionally.

"I'm listening," he insisted, his tone deep and seriously thick with an emotion of its own.

Reluctantly, Trenika pulled her hand away and shook her head, wrapping her arms around her as if she was afraid. She looked deeply into Josh's eyes and saw something in them that she knew to be cautious of. This wasn't that kid she had grown up with; he was all man now, strong and powerful, and in her heart of hearts, Trenika knew if she told him the truth it would definitely change the atmosphere between them.

"My heart is bleeding for you, Trenika. Please don't deny me the right to know what I should know to comfort a friend."

"You'll never understand," she repeated.

"Then, make me understand, goddammit!" He bristled, seeing the sorrow in her beautiful eyes.

Josh and she had fought many times back in the day, and Trenika always ended up getting her way. But this time, he was determined to win and by believing such, Josh got up and stepped around to sit down next to her and took Trenika into his arms. That's all it took to break her. Trenika sobbed and told him everything. He cried too, but those tears from him would come with a price; a price that would jeopardize the hearts of all those that mean the most to them. Kaedon was not going to like this. There was a problem.

There was a problem indeed, as Jourdan stared out the window of the family room at what was going on next door. At dawn that morning, big black SUV pulled up outside the safehouse and four all black clad figures emerged from the vehicle. The goon squad forced themselves through the front door of the safehouse with heavy artillery. After what seemed like an eternity, one single gunshot sounded off within the house. Next, the four armed goons piled back inside the SUV and sped away from the scene.

Sometime after nine o'clock that same morning, the secondary shift safehouse guard, Marco Purja, had arrived to find his partner dead, and hit the panic button. Before long, all types of law enforcement official showed up. Then, the CSI unit, the FBI, and the circus began. The disappearance of Al and his family had them all scratching their heads.

Jourdan and Al watched in silent dread as Nikolai was carted out in a black body bag and taken away. Then, the cops decided to go door to door questioning neighbors about what they might have or might not have witnessed. When the two cops showed up at Trenika's doorstep, Jourdan thought she was going into a panic attack, but she made sure everybody kept quiet and away from the windows in case one could look in and see them. Jourdan had them all bunched up in the master bedroom. As they listened intently at the continuous knocking at the front door. After about twenty minutes, Jourdan risked the opportunity to go check on what was going on next door.

"Oh Lord," Jourdan muttered.

There were more police outside than there was before. From somewhere down the hallway came the scratching sound of LuLu's clawing the bedroom door. Then, LuLu let out two gruff barks that sent Jourdan heading in its direction. Donecia peeped around the corner into the hallway and moved for LuLu's bedroom door. When she reached for the door handle, her wrist was clamped in a vise grip by her mother. Donecia looked up at her mother and saw the silent look of warning in her deep brown eyes.

"You definitely don't want to do that," said Jourdan.

"Why not?" Her daughter asked.

Jourdan shook her head and assured Donecia that releasing the dog right now just might be the worst decision she ever made. Then, Jourdan put her back against the door and slid down to a sitting position on the floor. The constant clawing ceased, and moments later there was a whimpering sound on the other side of the door.

"Mom, what are you doing?" Alex Jr, asked.

He too had come out into the hallway. Ignoring her son and daughter, Jourdan turned her face toward the crack of the door.

"It's okay, LuLu. We don't mean you no harm. I'm just here to keep my family safe. Trenika is my friend, and she welcomed us to come here. I wanna let you out to be with us, but we have to establish trust honey," she said in the softest voice that all members of her family knew to be without question that she means well.

Both of her children were looking at her as though she had lost her mind.

"We can be friends too, LuLu. Please don't hurt my family or me. I trust you, but I need you to trust me too, honey. I need you to protect us if need be."

"Mom, you're talking to a dog like it's human. It doesn't even understand what you are saying." Frowned Alex Jr.

Nodding her head solemnly, Jourdan said, "She understands very well," then she reached up to twist the door handle and pushed it open.

Still sitting down on the floor, her heart thudding in her chest; she sensed LuLu behind her and did not move a muscle. But Donecia and Alex Jr gasped in fright at the large dog and LuLu just stared out at them both. Then, the dog took two steps forward to come rest next to Jourdan. When she turned her head to look at the dog, both of their noses grazed the other. Then, LuLu tilted her large head and nudged the other woman affectionately.

"It's okay honey." Jourdan reached up and stroked the head of the beast before her.

From the doorway of the master bedroom, Al looked like he was ready to take flight. Then the dog turned away from them and headed toward the front of the house. This was LuLu's kingdom, and she roamed about the house to make sure all was well.

"Amazing," Alex Jr. finally spoke up. "Damn. Mom."

Donecia was speechless. The girl would have sworn the dog was about to attack all of them, but once again, her mother proved to be one of the most astonishing persons to ever be a part of her life.

Chapter 35

Tazzy turned out to be cool as hell, despite the circumstances of her not clicking too tight with Zamon. She was the type that dealt with others she could relate to someone who was cut from the cloth, but she admired Zamon's intelligence having conversed with him on a variety of subjects. He was a great conversationist, however, she clicked with Kaedon the most since they were of the same caliber.

Kaedon was intrigued with Tazzy's story with how she was brought up. The daughter of a legendary stripper and dancer, all Tazzy knew was the inside of strips clubs in the dressing rooms and parking lot hustling. Having also been brought up fatherless, she found all the male love in the form of street gangstas and hustlers. At eleven years old, Tazzy shot a man who believed to have been abusing her mother. Right there in the strip club in front of everybody, she stole the pistol from her mother's purse and committed her first crime.

At fifteen, Tazzy killed two young Inglewood Bloods who came to the house to trick off with her mother but had been scheming to rob her. Back then her mother, Stacy "Cinnamon" Williams was clocking at least five thousand a night at the club. Plus, she was making a killing selling pills and coke which led two jack boys to believe that they could enter her home and rob her for everything. That same night, Cinnamon was arrested for the killings of the two Bloods to save her daughter from getting in trouble. Mama had made the ultimate sacrifice and eventually paid the penalty of death for her actions. She was murdered in prison two days after her arrival.

Force to fend for herself, Tazzy relocated from Inglewood to Compton where she became the pride and joy of the Crip Nation. From then on it was a long tale of life in crime for Tazzy and her reputation became a thing to be admired.

The siblings had bonded that day and learned a lot about one another. As for the story of their father, it was a subject that Tazzy didn't care to discuss. Neither had the twins for that matter. What mattered the most was their mutual bonding. But when her presence was needed in her street affairs, Tazzy did not dare bring them along, instead she promised to meet up with them later. Having gotten to really know Tazzy in the very short time they'd been together, the twins didn't want their bonding to end, but Tazzy had other responsibilities that needed to be tended to. When they finally separated, it was damn near eight something and Kaedon was tired.

"She's nothing like Ciera," said Kaedon after Tazzy dropped them off back at their Aunt Amy's house.

"But I think they would get along quite well."

"She had a very troubling upbringing."

"Who hasn't?" Kaedon said looking over at his brother and noticing the obvious look on his face. "Except for you, Zee. At least you had both of your parents in the house. Then, you being the only child, you had it made."

"It wasn't always peaches and cream, Kaedon."

"Bullshit!" Kaedon said.

He took a seat down on the porch steps and began twisting up and blunt of weed. From inside the house an explosion of laughter sounded off as Amy entertained company. None of the usual gangstas posted up outside her home like the day before. But there was a lot of activity going on along the street. Old school cars with custom paint jobs and chrome rims went to and from along the street. Even a few Mexican lowriders rode through the set bumping some Bad Bunny and repping their true blue colors as well. The nightlife in Long Beach was a never-ending parade of gangsterism and nonstop entertainment.

"So, what is your conclusion of this whole journey, Kaedon?" Zamon wanted to know.

He stood leaning against the banister while facing his twin brother.

"That we came from a history of gangstaz."

"Really? That's your conclusion? To be frank, I agree, but if I had to choose between this life with my blood family or a life with my family back in Georgia, I would choose back home. I mean, what's more there is her than a life of crime and constantly looking over your shoulder every day? We deserve better than this Kaedon. Who's to say if we really did grow up here where would we be today?"

"I'll be the same nigga I am right now."

"You don't know that," said Zamon.

Kaedon put fire to his blunt. "This is my story, my calling, to be a gangsta and change people's lives…"

"By selling them drugs and killing them?" Zamon shook his head. "The only ending for a gangsta is either death of his own design or life in prison. I don't want that for you, Kaedon. Now that I know you and have you as a brother, Tazzy as well, I wouldn't want that for her too. For everybody else, that's their lives, that's the choice they made, but we are a family now and we must love, honor, and respect one another. I know being a gangsta is all you know, Kaedon. But does that gangsta in you care about the feelings of Ary and Trenika to the point that you can put it aside and focus on their happiness? What's the life of a gangsta when that gangsta would eventually break the hearts of those he love? Answer that for me, Kaedon. Is being a gangsta worth losing your family over?"

Zamon had definitely hit him where it hurt, and Kaedon couldn't deny the fact that he was right. Earlier when Kaedon first saw Tazzy, he wanted to get involved but knew that wasn't his place. Seeing her command the order of her team was thrilling; it reminded him of his own status. Being in the company of people of Naja, Von, and Tazzy's caliber always did something to him. He missed the days when he was out there running the streets and making niggas bleed. He had indeed sat his gangsta mentality aside to focus on family. If his twin had seen what he saw today that Kaedon would have loved to live in a place like Long Beach. That everyday gangsta shit was what kept him on his toes, but now as he reflects on his life and the things that Zamon had said, Kaedon knew that he still had a lot of work to do.

"I get it," said Kaedon.

Now he wanted to leave Cali and get back to his girl.

"All I'm really saying bro, is that we are blessed to be who we are today. Look where we have come from compared to where we could have been if our lives hadn't taken such a dramatic turn. Are you happy Kaedon?'

Kaedon was just asking himself the same question.

"I'm content," he said.

"Do you love Ary and Trenika?"

"You know I do." Kaedon looked at him like he was crazy.

"Then, love then and kill that gangsta shit. Be a man, twin brother. Not another statistic like the rest of them." With that being said, Zamon squeezed his shoulder and went into the house.

He was growing exhausted with the gangsta talk. Pulling on the blunt and inhaling weed smoke into his lungs, Kaedon looked out upon the night light surrounding him. You had gangstas hanging out on street corners and in their front yard. Gun shots sounded off somewhere in the distance. A seven-year-old kid was walking alongside of the curb aimlessly. Someone was blasting Nipsey Hussle from their sound system nearby. Kaedon, after taking all this in, knew this was the life that raised him, but was it the type of life he wanted for his own family? Wondered Kaedon.

"I wanna go home," he whispered, hearing police sirens blaring in the night. "But damn, how can one not love that gangsta shit?"

"I still can't get over it. Every time I think about it, I want to pinch myself to make sure it really happened." Lisa was saying to Trenika after calling to check up on things. She and Jhene was seated together in the porch swing that Grandma Cora had installed way before either one of them were born.

"It is, isn't it? This isn't a dream."

"You're the one with the big rock on your finger, Lisa. It feels good to me, so I know how much it must feel to you," said Trenika.

Next to her best friend, Jhene leaned against Trenika with her head on her shoulder, staring out into the night. Inside, Aryanna was stretched out on the living room floor asleep on a makeshift pallet of blankets and a comforter. The old lady was probably readying herself for bed as well.

"I'm punch drunk like a muthafucker, sis," Lisa said and laughed. "I've never felt so damn alive. Fuck it. I want babies too. A whole football team of little Bryons!" She blurted out animatedly.

"Now you're talking baby. I was wondering when you were gonna make me an auntie," Trenika said and Jhene yawned loudly, indicating that she was growing bored with the one-way conversation she was having, but that was before they spotted a lone figure coming down the sidewalk and entered the front yard.

By the glow of the moonlight overhead, it wasn't hard to tell it was Josh. After being gone for about three hours after his moment with Trenika earlier, he was back like he never left. Tonight, Josh was in a pair of basketball shorts, Air Jordan slides and a tank top that promoted his bulging muscles. At 6 foot even and weighing 220 lbs., Josh was far from the skinny kid he once was. In his hand, he carried a small brown paper bag. Watching him come near them, looking the way he did made Trenika's heart race. The man was dangerous, and she had already made that clear to him.

"Here we go," Jhene sat upright, and she watched Josh climb onto the porch.

"Hello ladies," he said. "I brought some snacks."

Then, he proceeded to reach into the bag and extracted a pack of Starburst candy for Trenika. It was her favorite candy during her childhood and even till this day. Then, he handed Jhene her favorite as well, which was Skittles, the ones in the green pack.

"Now, you done really showed your ass, Josh! Thank you," said Jhene, pleased that he remembered what her favorite candy was after all these years.

She remembered back when they were young when Josh used to go in their neighborhood convenience store and steal their favorite candy for them so that they wouldn't spend their money. Trenika, not wanting to blow her friend off on the phone, but she had to end her call with Lisa. Her attention was demanded by some delicious colorful candy and a man that still made her heart do strange things.

For Josh, he had chosen his beloved Star Crunch pastry and a Zebra Cake. When he was just a boy, he would literally eat a whole box of each pastry a day and not eat nothing else. Then, right there without even saying one word he devoured both pastries and laughed at the looks he received from both women.

"What?" He said with a sheepish grin.

"They don't feed you that stuff in the Marines?" Jhene asked.

"Not hardly," he said.

Trenika said, "Then, you better eat all you can eat now while you can."

That's when Josh looked her dead in the eyes and licked his big juicy lips anticipatingly.

"And that's exactly what I'm tryna do, Trenika. Eat. All. I. Can. Eat," he replied in a tone that made both women very uneasy.

Then, he burst out laughing and pointed at their faces, but Trenika wasn't laughing at all. She knew what he meant; it was clear in the way he looked at her. Joshua Freeman is a very dangerous being and if she wasn't careful, she would do something she knew she wouldn't ever forgive herself for. That was betraying Kaedon's trust and she damn sure wasn't trying to do that. Jhene looked over at her as though reading her current thoughts and shook her head.

"Josh," said Trenika in that voice that was meant for business. "There's something you must know," and with a deep breath she told her former love all about her new love, and once again, it was another blow to his heart.

Tonight, he had come to her with his heart in his hands only to have that same heart handed back to him. That's just the way it is. Her heart was already taken, and by a gangsta who had changed her whole life.

Chapter 36

The following day, the twins ate a big breakfast with their extended family, went shopping with Tazzy that morning, had lunch with Tazzy and Sasha, and was on a flight to New Orleans at 1:00 that afternoon. But not without promising to visit again or vice versa. Because they couldn't just leave their newfound family without some type of insurance. When they finally reached New Orleans later on that evening, Lance had already made the trip, and he came to scoop them up without question. Trenika had no clue that Kaedon had decided to come at that time. He wanted to surprise her, but not tonight. The twins will sleep over at Lance's place and visit tomorrow. There was no way Kaedon would interrupt the peace of Grandma Cora at such a late hour of the night. The plan was to start afresh and with a grand entrance.

Lance had a nice penthouse apartment overlooking the city with an amazing view. The life of a gangsta was certainly doing well for Lance. Elegant and casually decorated, he had put much thought into the detail of his pad. The place showed a lot about his character and from the looks of it Lance was very artistic when it came down to interior designing, one would never have expected to come from a young black street thug. Kaedon guessed artists ran deep in their family.

That night while laying awake in the guest room waiting on the next sunrise, Kaedon thought about his life with

Trenika and what it meant to him. That morning, he had spent almost fifteen thousand dollars on a ring for his woman. Although it was more of Tazzy's liking, he knew that once Trenika sees it, it's going to blow her mind. Kaedon felt good about what he was about to do. He was confident the choice he was making was right. Marrying Trenika was the only way he could ensure her his love forever. She was that forever type of woman. Trenika was worth all the diamond rings in the world. She was a diamond of her own. A diamond in the rough that he found and plans to cherish for all it's worth.

Checking the time on his watch and seeing that it was 1:19 AM, Kaedon smirked and reached for his phone. He hit the phone number on speed dial. When the answering machine came on, he called the number again. He had to share his thoughts with somebody, he needed some attention.

"This shit better be damn good calling my damn house in the middle of the gotdamn night," Old man Jake grouchily answered the phone.

"I'm going to do it, Jake. I'm gonna marry her. I bought the ring today. Well, on yesterday. I'm ready."

"Son…" Jake paused for a moment. "I'm happy for you, son. You chose wisely, my boy. But do me a favor though," he replied.

"What is it?" Kaedon sat up in bed.

"Call me when it's time to fit my tuxedo," Jake said and hung up the phone on his ear.

Kaedon laughed to himself, but that was all the clarification he needed. He indeed was doing the right thing by making his woman his legal wife.

"Trenika Denise Smith," muttered Kaedon trying out Trenika's name with his. "Damn that shit sounds good."

"Go to bed, Kaed!" Zamon yelled at him from across the hall and once again. Kaedon laughed out loud.

He couldn't help himself, he was in love, and he was about to do something that he once told himself he would never do. Let a woman tie him down, but it was the other way around for him; for he was planning to tie her down first. Do it before it was too late, before the next man does.

When morning came, Trenika was awakened by Aryanna and she demanded to go to school. The child wanted to go be with her friends, but Trenika had to remind her that there wasn't no school that day. It was a holiday. It was Labor Day, which Trenika had to explain the meaning of. Aryanna still wasn't trying to hear that and left the room in a funk.

Trenika got out of bed, handled her morning rituals, and entered the kitchen to find her grandmother sitting down at the table nursing a cup of coffee. Obviously, Aryanna had beat her up and had already eaten her breakfast, which was a bowl of cereal.

"Morning, Mama." Trenika greeted the old lady with a gentle kiss upon her cheek.

"You slept with the angels last night, my dear?"

"Yes, I did," she smiled.

"Well," Grandma Cora sat her cup down in front of her. "I have to be at a Senior's Club House this morning to help prepare for the big event I told you about. Donna Mae should be here at any minute now to pick me up. You are welcome to drop by for a spell if you're up to it. You remember Donna Mae, right?" She asked.

"The one with the crooked eyes."

How could she forget the old lady smells like mothballs and mouthwash. Grandma Cora swatted at Trenika's arm and smacked her for trying to rank on her old friend, but it surely didn't keep her from blushing though.

"Don't talk about Donna Mae like that. We've been friends for over fifty years now, and we're still standing strong till this day, dear."

"The last of a dying breed," remarked Trenika.

"Who's dying," Aryanna said stepping into the kitchen and taking a seat at the table.

"Nobody's dying child," said her great-grandmother. "If anything, we'll still be here a hundred years from now."

"I wanna live a hundred years," Aryanna said.

The old lady smiled over at the little girl and said that she would live to see more than that if she took good care of herself and said her prayers. There was a knock at the front door and Trenika excused herself to go answer it. For an instant, she was expecting it to be Josh, especially after what happened last night. Once again, she had bruised his pride by declaring her love for another man when he expected to at least try to reclaim what he have never let go years ago. He slunk back home without a goodbye or goodnight. So, she did expect him to come to try his luck again after going home to plan a greater act of persuasion. That's what the younger Josh would have done. He expected too much out of what he still feels is rightfully his but isn't. Josh would just have to respect her mind. She was taken already.

When Trenika finally made it to the door, she opened it and damn near fainted where she stood.

"I don't know how long is forever, but I'm willing to make it there with you as my wife. I know that you will make it possible for me to fall in love with you over and over everyday. I'd wake up with you on my side and as your husband, I promise to do the same and more. I never love another woman like I love you, Trenika. You are the perfect match for me, and I will prove it to you every day until I take my last breath. Will you marry me?" Kaedon was already down on one knee when she opened the door. And in his outstretched hand with a huge diamond ring that sparkled with brilliancy.

"Please say yes," he replied.

Trenika stood there with tears pouring from her eyes that she stared at the man she loved more than life itself. Behind him, standing at the curb with all of her friends and family, everybody having shown up for the occasion of the proposal.

Somehow, Kaedon had set this up without her knowing and it was a very surprising performance.

"You've made me out of a believer, baby. I never knew true love until you pulled me out of the rain that day. I knew the moment I first laid eyes on you that you'll be mine forever. I knew it, Trenika. So right now, I am proving just now how serious I am," he professed.

"No..." Trenika sobbed. "I can't."

"Huh?" Kaedon paused. "No?"

Trenika shook her head and turned around and ran away from him, leaving Kaedon staring after her, looking lost and confused. And it was then, for the third time in his whole life, he felt scared and afraid. What had he done? Thought Kaedon. Little did he know it wasn't about what he did, but what Trenika saw just now.

Romell was back again.

To Be Continued...

Lock Down Publications and Ca$h Presents
Assisted Publishing Packages

Due to an increase in the price of services we have increased our prices. The prices below reflect the price increase as of 11/1/24.

BASIC PACKAGE	UPGRADED PACKAGE
$699	**$1000**
Editing	Typing
Cover Design	Editing
Formatting	Cover Design
	Formatting
	Upload eBooks to Amazon
	Upload Paperback to Amazon
ADVANCE PACKAGE	**LDP SUPREME PACKAGE**
$1,400	**$1,700**
Typing	Typing
Editing (line editing/content)	Editing (line editing/content)
Cover Design	Cover Design
Formatting	Formatting
Copyright Registration	Copyright Registration
Proofreading	Proofreading
Upload eBooks to Amazon	Set up Amazon Account
Upload Paperback to Amazon	Upload eBooks to Amazon
	Upload Paperback to Amazon
	Advertise on LDP's Amazon and Facebook Page

***Other services available upon request.
Additional charges may apply

Lock Down Publications
P.O. Box 944
Stockbridge, GA 30281-9998
Phone: 470 303-9761
Email: lockdownpublications@gmail.com

Submission Guideline

Submit the first three chapters of your completed manuscript to ldpsubmissions@gmail.com. In the subject line add **Your Book's Title**. The manuscript must be in a Word Doc file and sent as an attachment. Document should be in Times New Roman, double spaced, and in size 12 font. Also, provide your synopsis and full contact information. If sending multiple submissions, they must each be in a separate email.

Have a story but no way to send it electronically? You can still submit to LDP/Ca$h Presents. Send in the first three chapters, written or typed, of your completed manuscript to:

LDP: Submissions Dept
P.O. Box 944
Stockbridge, GA 30281-9998

DO NOT send original manuscript. Must be a duplicate. Provide your synopsis and a cover letter containing your full contact information.

Thanks for considering LDP and Ca$h Presents.

NEW RELEASES

BLOODLINE OF A SAVAGE 1&2
THESE VICIOUS STREETS 1&2
RELENTLESS GOON
RELENTLESS GOON 2
BY PRINCE A. TAUHID

THE BUTTERFLY MAFIA 1-3
BY FUMIYA PAYNE

A THUG'S STREET PRINCESS 1&2
BY MEESHA

CITY OF SMOKE 2
BY MOLOTTI

STEPPERS 1,2&3
THE REAL BADDIES OF CHI-RAQ
BY KING RIO

THE LANE 1&2
BY KEN-KEN SPENCE

THUG OF SPADES 1&2
LOVE IN THE TRENCHES 2
CORNER BOYS
BY COREY ROBINSON

TIL DEATH 3
BY ARYANNA

THE BIRTH OF A GANGSTER 4
BY DELMONT PLAYER

PRODUCT OF THE STREETS 1&2
BY DEMOND "MONEY" ANDERSON

NO TIME FOR ERROR
BY KEESE

MONEY HUNGRY DEMONS
BY TRANAY ADAMS

Coming Soon from Lock Down Publications/Ca$h Presents

IF YOU CROSS ME ONCE 6
ANGEL V
By Anthony Fields

IMMA DIE BOUT MINE 5
By Aryanna

A THUGS STREET PRINCESS 3
By Meesha

PRODUCT OF THE STREETS 3
By Demond Money Anderson

CORNER BOYS 2
By Corey Robinson

THE MURDER QUEENS 6&7
By Michael Gallon

CITY OF SMOKE 3
By Molotti

CONFESSIONS OF A DOPE BOY
By Nicholas Lock

THA TAKEOVER
By Keith Chandler

BETRAYAL OF A G 2
By Ray Vinci

CRIME BOSS
By Playa Ray

Available Now

RESTRAINING ORDER 1 & 2
By **CA$H & Coffee**

LOVE KNOWS NO BOUNDARIES 1-3
By **Coffee**

RAISED AS A GOON I, II, III & IV
BRED BY THE SLUMS I, II, III
BLAST FOR ME I & II
ROTTEN TO THE CORE I II III
A BRONX TALE I, II, III
DUFFLE BAG CARTEL I II III IV V VI
HEARTLESS GOON I II III IV V
A SAVAGE DOPEBOY I II
DRUG LORDS I II III
CUTTHROAT MAFIA I II
KING OF THE TRENCHES
By **Ghost**

LAY IT DOWN I & II
LAST OF A DYING BREED I II
BLOOD STAINS OF A SHOTTA I & II III
By **Jamaica**

LOYAL TO THE GAME I II III
LIFE OF SIN I, II III
By **TJ & Jelissa**

IF LOVING HIM IS WRONG…I & II
LOVE ME EVEN WHEN IT HURTS I II III
By **Jelissa**

PUSH IT TO THE LIMIT
By **Bre' Hayes**

A THUGGISH PASSION | IRA B

BLOODY COMMAS I & II
SKI MASK CARTEL I, II & III
KING OF NEW YORK I II, III IV V
RISE TO POWER I II III
COKE KINGS I II III IV V
BORN HEARTLESS I II III IV
KING OF THE TRAP I II
By **T.J. Edwards**

WHEN THE STREETS CLAP BACK I & II III
THE HEART OF A SAVAGE I II III IV
MONEY MAFIA I II
LOYAL TO THE SOIL I II III
By **Jibril Williams**

A DISTINGUISHED THUG STOLE MY HEART I II & III
LOVE SHOULDN'T HURT I II III IV
RENEGADE BOYS 1-4
PAID IN KARMA 1-3
SAVAGE STORMS 1-3
AN UNFORESEEN LOVE 1-3
BABY, I'M WINTERTIME COLD 1-3
A THUG'S STREET PRINCESS 1&2
By **Meesha**

A GANGSTER'S CODE 1-3
A GANGSTER'S SYN 1-3
THE SAVAGE LIFE 1-3
CHAINED TO THE STREETS 1-3
BLOOD ON THE MONEY 1-3
A GANGSTA'S PAIN 1-3
BEAUTIFUL LIES AND UGLY TRUTHS
CHURCH IN THESE STREETS
By **J-Blunt**

CUM FOR ME 1-8
An LDP Erotica Collaboration

A THUGGISH PASSION | IRA B

BLOOD OF A BOSS 1-5
SHADOWS OF THE GAME
TRAP BASTARD
By **Askari**

THE STREETS BLEED MURDER 1-3
THE HEART OF A GANGSTA 1-3
By **Jerry Jackson**

WHEN A GOOD GIRL GOES BAD
By **Adrienne**

THE COST OF LOYALTY 1-3
By **Kweli**

BRIDE OF A HUSTLA 1-3
THE FETTI GIRLS 1-3
CORRUPTED BY A GANGSTA 1-4
BLINDED BY HIS LOVE
THE PRICE YOU PAY FOR LOVE 1-3
DOPE GIRL MAGIC 1-3
By **Destiny Skai**

A KINGPIN'S AMBITION
A KINGPIN'S AMBITION II
I MURDER FOR THE DOUGH
By **Ambitious**

TRUE SAVAGE 1-7
DOPE BOY MAGIC 1-3
MIDNIGHT CARTEL 1-3
CITY OF KINGZ 1&2
NIGHTMARE ON SILENT AVE
THE PLUG OF LIL MEXICO 1&2
CLASSIC CITY
By **Chris Green**

A THUGGISH PASSION | IRA B

A GANGSTER'S REVENGE 1-4
THE BOSS MAN'S DAUGHTERS 1-5
A SAVAGE LOVE 1&2
BAE BELONGS TO ME 1&2
A HUSTLER'S DECEIT 1-3
WHAT BAD BITCHES DO 1-3
SOUL OF A MONSTER 1-3
KILL ZONE
A DOPE BOY'S QUEEN 1-3
TIL DEATH 1-3
IMMA DIE BOUT MINE 1-4
By **Aryanna**

A DOPEBOY'S PRAYER
By **Eddie "Wolf" Lee**

THE KING CARTEL 1-3
By **Frank Gresham**

THESE NIGGAS AIN'T LOYAL 1-3
By **Nikki Tee**

GANGSTA SHYT 1-3
By **CATO**

THE ULTIMATE BETRAYAL
By **Phoenix**

BOSS'N UP 1-3
By **Royal Nicole**

I LOVE YOU TO DEATH
By **Destiny J**

I RIDE FOR MY HITTA
I STILL RIDE FOR MY HITTA
By **Misty Holt**

LOVE & CHASIN' PAPER
By **Qay Crockett**

TO DIE IN VAIN
SINS OF A HUSTLA
By **ASAD**

BROOKLYN HUSTLAZ
By **Boogsy Morina**

BROOKLYN ON LOCK 1 & 2
By **Sonovia**

GANGSTA CITY
By **Teddy Duke**

A DRUG KING AND HIS DIAMOND 1-3
A DOPEMAN'S RICHES
HER MAN, MINE'S TOO 1&2
CASH MONEY HO'S
THE WIFEY I USED TO BE 1&2
PRETTY GIRLS DO NASTY THINGS
By **Nicole Goosby**

LIPSTICK KILLAH 1-3
CRIME OF PASSION 1-3
FRIEND OR FOE 1-3
By **Mimi**

TRAPHOUSE KING 1-3
KINGPIN KILLAZ 1-3
STREET KINGS 1&2
PAID IN BLOOD 1&2
CARTEL KILLAZ 1-3
DOPE GODS 1&2
By **Hood Rich**

THE STREETS ARE CALLING
By **Duquie Wilson**

STEADY MOBBN' 1-3
THE STREETS STAINED MY SOUL 1-3
By **Marcellus Allen**

WHO SHOT YA 1-3
SON OF A DOPE FIEND 1-4
HEAVEN GOT A GHETTO 1&2
SKI MASK MONEY 1&2
By **Renta**

GORILLAZ IN THE BAY 1-4
TEARS OF A GANGSTA 1/&2
3X KRAZY 1&2
STRAIGHT BEAST MODE 1&2
By **DE'KARI**

TRIGGADALE 1-3
MURDA WAS THE CASE 1-3
By **Elijah R. Freeman**

SLAUGHTER GANG 1-3
RUTHLESS HEART 1-3
By **Willie Slaughter**

GOD BLESS THE TRAPPERS 1-3
THESE SCANDALOUS STREETS 1-3
FEAR MY GANGSTA 1-5
THESE STREETS DON'T LOVE NOBODY 1-2
BURY ME A G 1-5
A GANGSTA'S EMPIRE 1-4
THE DOPEMAN'S BODYGAURD 1&2
THE REALEST KILLAZ 1-3
THE LAST OF THE OGS 1-3
By **Tranay Adams**

MARRIED TO A BOSS 1-3
By **Destiny Skai & Chris Green**

KINGZ OF THE GAME 1-7
CRIME BOSS 1-3
By **Playa Ray**

FUK SHYT
By **Blakk Diamond**

DON'T F#CK WITH MY HEART 1&2
By **Linnea**

ADDICTED TO THE DRAMA 1-3
IN THE ARM OF HIS BOSS
By **Jamila**

LOYALTY AIN'T PROMISED 1&2
By **Keith Williams**

YAYO 1-4
A SHOOTER'S AMBITION 1&2
BRED IN THE GAME
By **S. Allen**

TRAP GOD 1-3
RICH $AVAGE 1-3
MONEY IN THE GRAVE 1-3
CARTEL MONEY
By **Martell Troublesome Bolden**

FOREVER GANGSTA 1&2
GLOCKS ON SATIN SHEETS 1&2
By **Adrian Dulan**

TOE TAGZ 1-4
LEVELS TO THIS SHYT 1&2
IT'S JUST ME AND YOU
By **Ah'Million**

A THUGGISH PASSION | IRA B

KINGPIN DREAMS 1-3
RAN OFF ON DA PLUG
By **Paper Boi Rari**

THE STREETS MADE ME 1-3
By **Larry D. Wright**

CONFESSIONS OF A GANGSTA 1-4
CONFESSIONS OF A JACKBOY 1-3
CONFESSIONS OF A HITMAN
By **Nicholas Lock**

I'M NOTHING WITHOUT HIS LOVE
SINS OF A THUG
TO THE THUG I LOVED BEFORE
A GANGSTA SAVED XMAS
IN A HUSTLER I TRUST
By **Monet Dragun**

QUIET MONEY 1-3
THUG LIFE 1-3
EXTENDED CLIP 1&2
A GANGSTA'S PARADISE
By **Trai'Quan**

CAUGHT UP IN THE LIFE 1-3
THE STREETS NEVER LET GO 1-3
By **Robert Baptiste**

NEW TO THE GAME 1-3
MONEY, MURDER & MEMORIES 1-3
By **Malik D. Rice**

CREAM 2-3
THE STREETS WILL TALK
By **Yolanda Moore**

THE STREETS WILL NEVER CLOSE 1-3
By **K'ajji**

LIFE OF A SAVAGE 1-4
A GANGSTA'S QUR'AN 1-4
MURDA SEASON 1-3
GANGLAND CARTEL 1-3
CHI'RAQ GANGSTAS 1-4
KILLERS ON ELM STREET 1-3
JACK BOYZ N DA BRONX 1-3
A DOPEBOY'S DREAM 1-3
JACK BOYS VS DOPE BOYS 1-3
COKE GIRLZ
COKE BOYS
SOSA GANG 1&2
BRONX SAVAGES
BODYMORE KINGPINS
BLOOD OF A GOON
By **Romell Tukes**

CONCRETE KILLA 1-3
VICIOUS LOYALTY 1-3
By **Kingpen**

THE ULTIMATE SACRIFICE 1-6
KHADIFI
IF YOU CROSS ME ONCE 1-3
ANGEL 1-4
IN THE BLINK OF AN EYE
By **Anthony Fields**

THE LIFE OF A HOOD STAR
By **Ca$h & Rashia Wilson**

NIGHTMARES OF A HUSTLA 1-3
BLOOD AND GAMES 1&2
By **King Dream**

GHOST MOB
By **Stilloan Robinson**

HARD AND RUTHLESS 1&2
MOB TOWN 251
THE BILLIONAIRE BENTLEYS 1-3
REAL G'S MOVE IN SILENCE
By **Von Diesel**

MOB TIES 1-7
SOUL OF A HUSTLER, HEART OF A KILLER 1-3
GORILLAZ IN THE TRENCHES
By **SayNoMore**

BODYMORE MURDERLAND 1-3
THE BIRTH OF A GANGSTER 1-4
By **Delmont Player**

FOR THE LOVE OF A BOSS 1&2
By **C. D. Blue**

KILLA KOUNTY 1-5
By **Khufu**

MOBBED UP 1-4
THE BRICK MAN 1-5
THE COCAINE PRINCESS 1-10
STEPPERS 1-3
SUPER GREMLIN 1-4
By **King Rio**

MONEY GAME 1&2
By **Smoove Dolla**

A GANGSTA'S KARMA 1-4
By **FLAME**

KING OF THE TRENCHES 1-3
By **GHOST & TRANAY ADAMS**

A THUGGISH PASSION | IRA B

QUEEN OF THE ZOO 1&2
By **Black Migo**

GRIMEY WAYS 1-3
BETRAYAL OF A G
By **Ray Vinci**

XMAS WITH AN ATL SHOOTER
By **Ca$h & Destiny Skai**

KING KILLA 1&2
By **Vincent "Vitto" Holloway**

BETRAYAL OF A THUG 1&2
By **Fre$h**

THE MURDER QUEENS 1-5
By **Michael Gallon**

FOR THE LOVE OF BLOOD 1-4
By **Jamel Mitchell**

HOOD CONSIGLIERE 1&2
NO TIME FOR ERROR
By **Keese**

PROTÉGÉ OF A LEGEND 1&2
LOVE IN THE TRENCHES 1&2
By **Corey Robinson**

THE PLUG'S RUTHLESS DAUGHTER
By **Tony Daniels**

BORN IN THE GRAVE 1-3
CRIME PAYS
By **Self Made Tay**

MOAN IN MY MOUTH
By **XTASY**

TORN BETWEEN A GANGSTER AND A GENTLEMAN
By **J-BLUNT & Miss Kim**

LOYALTY IS EVERYTHING 1-3
CITY OF SMOKE 1&2
By **Molotti**

HERE TODAY GONE TOMORROW 1&2
By **Fly Rock**

WOMEN LIE MEN LIE 1-4
FIFTY SHADES OF SNOW 1-3
STACK BEFORE YOU SPLURGE
GIRLS FALL LIKE DOMINOES
NAÏVE TO THE STREETS
By **ROY MILLIGAN**

PILLOW PRINCESS
By **S. Hawkins**

THE BUTTERFLY MAFIA 1-3
SALUTE MY SAVAGERY 1&2
By **Fumiya Payne**

THE LANE 1&2
By Ken-Ken Spence

THE PUSSY TRAP 1-5
By **Nene Capri**

DIRTY DNA
By **Blaque**

SANCTIFIED AND HORNY
by **XTASY**

BOOKS BY LDP'S CEO, CA$H

TRUST IN NO MAN
TRUST IN NO MAN 2
TRUST IN NO MAN 3
BONDED BY BLOOD
SHORTY GOT A THUG
THUGS CRY
THUGS CRY 2
THUGS CRY 3
TRUST NO BITCH
TRUST NO BITCH 2
TRUST NO BITCH 3
TIL MY CASKET DROPS
RESTRAINING ORDER
RESTRAINING ORDER 2
IN LOVE WITH A CONVICT
LIFE OF A HOOD STAR
XMAS WITH AN ATL SHOOTER

www.ingramcontent.com/pod-product-compliance
Lightning Source LLC
Chambersburg PA
CBHW071149260626
47162CB00003B/972